ADAM WINS THE INTERNET

'Brilliant, enticing and leaves you wanting more' –
Kirsty, Amazon reviewer

'This is definitely a must-read book, just don't
expect hot drinks to stay hot cos you'll be so
absorbed in what you're reading that the time
will just slip by' – Amanda G., NetGalley
reviewer

'A really good read for someone who
is starting to navigate the internet
themselves' – Ejwal, Toppsta reviewer

'It was one of those books when all the
children laughed at the same time' –
teacher review, NetGalley

'This is a touchingly human story,
tremendously funny, glittering with
authenticity and a wonderful thing to
connect with' – Tesse, NetGalley reviewer

'This is the best book I've ever read in my life' –
Andrew, Amazon reviewer

ADAM WINS THE INTERNET

ADAM B

Illustrated by **JAMES LANCETT**

BLOOMSBURY
CHILDREN'S BOOKS
LONDON   OXFORD   NEW YORK   NEW DELHI   SYDNEY

BLOOMSBURY CHILDREN'S BOOKS
Bloomsbury Publishing Plc
50 Bedford Square, London WC1B 3DP, UK
29 Earlsfort Terrace, Dublin 2, Ireland

BLOOMSBURY, BLOOMSBURY CHILDREN'S BOOKS and the Diana logo are
trademarks of Bloomsbury Publishing Plc

First published in Great Britain in 2022 by Bloomsbury Publishing Plc
This edition published in Great Britain in 2023 by Bloomsbury Publishing Plc

A catalogue record for this book is available from the British Library

ISBN: PB: 978-1-5266-5566-0; HB: 978-1-5266-5565-3; TPB: 978-1-5266-5564-6;
Waterstones: 978-1-5266-6810-3; eBook: 978-1-5266-5562-2; ePDF: 978-1-5266-5563-9

2 4 6 8 10 9 7 5 3 1

Typeset by RefineCatch Limited, Bungay, Suffolk

Printed and bound in Great Britain by CPI Group (UK) Ltd, Croydon CR0 4YY

To find out more about our authors and books visit
www.bloomsbury.com and sign up for our newsletters

To my mum and dad.

They believed in me so that I could believe in myself

1

The Heroes

It was morning. Not just any morning – Adam's favourite kind:

- Sunny (for October)
- Warm (except his feet, which at age thirteen no longer fitted in the bed he'd had since he was eight)
- Lazy. Slow enough for him to gather his thoughts, try to remember his dreams, plan which YouTubers to catch up on first …
- And best of all, it was the weekend. Nothing beats a long, relaxing lie-in on a Sunday mor—

'ADAM! You better be out of bed! We're leaving in ten minutes!'

Let's start again.

It was morning. Not just any morning. Adam's least favourite kind – the kind when you think it's the weekend, when actually it's a

MONDAY!

Adam had never literally leaped out of bed before, but there's a first time for everything. He had never tried to get both his gangly legs into his school jumper, or tried to brush his teeth with the handle of his toothbrush before, but hey, give him a break, he had been a teenager for a whole six weeks now, and teenagers are supposed to be rubbish at getting up in the morning, right?

'Oh, so you *are* alive?' his frazzled-looking mum managed to joke as Adam launched himself down the stairs and did a sock-slide into the kitchen, where his mum and brother were hurriedly finishing up breakfast.

His mum grabbed her keys from the side and began making for the front door, but she didn't get far before Adam had hold of her and was spinning her around

the kitchen, doing one of his 'dances', while singing one of his 'songs'. The dance in question was an Adam classic, and mostly involved him jumping around in circles. The song was also an Adam original, and, like all his other songs, consisted of two words, bellowed in what can only be described as a 'non-tune'.

'Ohhhh … Weeeee're … late, we're late. We're late, we're late, we're laaaate!'

It was common for Adam to try to irritate his mum when she was already on the verge of erupting into a full-on, code red, fury extravaganza. You'd think that it would be the final straw for her, but in fact, weirdly enough, it almost never failed to make her laugh. Making people happy, even when 'happy' seemed like a million miles away, was one of Adam's greatest skills. He was a world-class cheerer-upper. Or, as his mum put it –

'You're a whirlwind of annoyingness, that's what you are!' she yelled between howls of laughter. 'Now pack it in before you make us so late that you get detention and I get fired.'

'Nice hair, Adam,' mocked Adam's brother between huge mouthfuls of toast. Callum was only two years younger than Adam, but he looked *four* years younger, acted *eight* years younger, and was a genuine contender for Adam's title of 'Whirlwind of Annoyingness No. 1'. And Adam couldn't have been prouder of that.

'How long did it take you to make it look like you just got out of bed?' chuckled Callum as he stretched his arm up in an attempt to reach all the way to the top of Adam's stratospheric head, to mess up his shock of bed-hair even more.

'Probably about as long as it took you to make

your face look like it just got pushed out of a pig's bum,' quipped Adam.

'Adam!' his mum gasped. 'Too far!'

But Callum didn't think it was too far at all – he was chuckling toast out from between his teeth, and high-fiving his big brother in recognition of the funniest put-down of the day so far.

'Seriously, though,' said Callum, once he'd finally regained his composure, 'you need to sort your hair out. You look like Mum after the time we put glue in her shampoo!'

Now it was Adam's turn to get gross with the toast. It sprayed all over the kitchen floor as he doubled over at the memory of that day.

'Her face!' He howled with laughter as he played the moment back in his mind. 'When she opened the bathroom door – her *hair* – I've never seen anyone so shocked!'

'Oh, not shocked,' his mum corrected him, '*furious*. Which is exactly what I'll be in five seconds' time if you don't get a move on!'

They had fifteen minutes before they would be marked as being officially late for school, and Mum had one hour and fifteen minutes before she'd be late for work, so Adam knew they weren't really in any serious danger. But Mum never saw it that way. All Mum saw was the multiple things that could go wrong to slow them down on their way.

Like, for instance, their car, which today took five attempts to splutter to life before choking to a standstill at the end of the road.

The false start reminded Adam to dig in his pocket, fish out the 40p change from yesterday's lunch money and pop it into the cardboard box he'd wedged between the two front seats three months ago. It was a shoebox, with the lid taped on, a coin slot cut into

the top and the words 'New Gearbox Fund' scrawled across it in purple marker pen.

They'd only had the car for four months, after their old car – the beloved 'Dadmobile' – was stolen from outside their house. Mum thought she'd found a real bargain with the used Ford Focus. The ad had read – '*New tyres, new brakes, new gearbox!*' so she spent every last penny on it. Sadly, after getting the car home, she discovered that the advert hadn't listed all the things the car *had*, it was a list of all the things the car *needed*.

A new gearbox was right at the top of that list, but, at six hundred pounds, they were a loooooong way from being able to afford it. Luckily Adam had the problem under control – so far his 'New Gearbox Fund' idea had raised a whopping twelve pounds and twenty pence!

'Listen to all that money!' Adam gasped in mock amazement as he gave the box a shake. 'Not long to go now, Mum! This time in three years we'll be halfway saved up!'

'Adam, don't even joke,' his mum groaned, knowing he was probably right. 'I've had enough of this horrible old banger!'

It was a sentence that Adam struggled to make sense of. OK, he knew that, to Mum, a 'banger' was an out-of-date, unreliable car, like the Ford Focus they were sitting in, which was two years older than Adam, and was presently making a noise like an asthmatic donkey. But to Adam, a 'banger' was YouTube slang for a video that was an unstoppable, runaway, viral mega-hit. In Adam's mind a 'banger' was an amazing thing, not something that could ever be used in the same sentence as the words 'horrible' and 'old'.

And a 'banger' was what he was watching right now. (Or trying to watch – his phone was almost as useless as their car. It was bashed and beaten, with a camera that barely worked, and was five models out of date. But Adam was grateful for it, all the same. He knew his mum struggled to pay the six-pound bill every month, but he made sure it was money well spent.

His phone was a window to another world, a window that he gazed through for hours each day, where no matter how down, or stressed, or worried he was feeling, there was always someone like him – another world-class-cheerer-upper – uploading content that would put a smile back on Adam's face. Through the window of his phone he could escape to the land of TikTok, surf the waters of Instagram, and, best of all, explore the endless realms of YouTube – a place where he dreamed he might one day migrate to and become a fully certified citizen. To be a YouTuber was Adam's greatest dream – a dream where he could follow in the footsteps of all his favourite YouTubers and deliver his cheering-up skills not just to his mum and Callum, but to *millions* of people across the globe. *Just imagine making that many people happy*, he marvelled to himself.)

His favourite YouTuber, Ed Almighty, had posted a new video overnight, and even though Adam could only watch a few seconds at a time between bufferings, it was still one of the funniest things he had ever seen.

'I seriously don't understand what all the hype is about that guy,' groaned Callum, trying to lean himself forward from the back seat enough to see Adam's stuttering screen. 'He's so overrated. He didn't deserve *any* of those awards he got at WebCon last year!'

For the online community, WebCon was like the Oscars. It was where every web-fan like Adam dreamed of going. Adam would have especially loved to go last year, when Ed Almighty was the star of the show. Callum wasn't a massive fan of Ed Almighty. He was more into Jack-OJ.

Adam thought they were *both* heroes.

'Adam, you could be a better YouTuber than Ed Almighty without even trying! I'm not even joking!'

'Ha!' Adam laughed as he reached a hand back to give Callum an affectionate hair-ruffle, like he was an obedient puppy. 'You're a good little brother, Callum, you know that? Yesh you are! Yesh you *are*! Who's a good boy? You are!'

While Adam appreciated Callum's compliment, he knew that Callum was very, very wrong about him. Sure, Adam would have loved to be a YouTuber. There was nothing in the world he wanted to do more! That's what that glue-shampoo prank on his mum had been all about – it was practice! He and Callum had made *dozens* of YouTube videos. But that's all they ever were – 'practice' videos, which sat on Adam's hard drive and had never even so much as sniffed the band-width of a journey to the realms of YouTube.

The dream was never going to happen, and Adam knew it. And it wasn't just because his ancient laptop took all night to upload a five-minute video, and it wasn't because the camera on his brick of a phone was half dead. It was because there was something about Adam that Callum didn't know. Something that Adam didn't *want* Callum to know. A 'secondary school something'. Something that, if he ever found it out, would change Callum's opinion of Adam forever. And now that Callum was in his last year of primary school, and would join Adam's secondary school next year, Adam knew it was only a matter of time before his secret came out.

2

The Secret

Adam was grateful that, for now at least, his secret was safe. He didn't know how he would handle it if Callum ever found out ... *when* Callum found out. He didn't dare think about it – the shame, the disappointment ... Adam wished he could scrunch his eyes up, make fists with his hands and force the truth down a rabbit hole, all the way to the centre of the earth, where it would burn up and never be seen again. But this secret wasn't going anywhere. It was always there, hanging over him like his own personal storm cloud, always threatening to drench him in shame.

Mum stopped the car outside Callum's school, which was just a short walk down the road from

Adam's. Adam and Callum kissed Mum goodbye, and Callum gave her an extra squeeze as he leaned in from the back seat.

'See you later, Adam. Bye, Mum. Love you.'

'Bye-bye, sweetheart. Love you one m——' Mum paused and glanced at Adam, almost as if asking him permission to say the words they both knew Callum so longed to hear, but Adam pretended to be too busy getting out of the car to notice. So instead Mum went with the best alternative. 'Love you *so* much.'

Adam knew they weren't the exact words Callum had been hoping for, not like what Dad used to say, but they would have to do.

Callum was through the school doors in twelve seconds flat. And six minutes later Adam was approaching the side entrance doors of his own school. He hated those doors. The closer Adam got, the more his secret rumbled overhead. The second he passed through them, the cloud over his head would give a thunderous *BOOM* and his secret would rain down on him, making his transformation complete. Just like how the Hulk's secret is unleashed by anger, and Rogue's secret is activated whenever she touches

13

someone, Adam's secret was activated by those double doors round the side of his school. Except, when Adam stepped through them, he didn't become one of the Avengers or the X-Men. No, Adam's secret was different. When Adam stepped though those doors he became ...

'LOSER!'

The insults, the jeering, the mocking laughter — they all came barrelling towards him the second he was inside school. As usual, Bruce Kilter and his gang had been waiting for him.

Gone was the dancing Adam. No more singing. No more laughing toast all over the floor. When Adam was in school he became a completely different person. Head down, eyes down, don't talk, try to be invisible – those were Adam's four rules of survival, and some days they actually helped him avoid being noticed by Bruce and his hangers-on.

Today was not one of those days.

'Oi, loser! Don't ignore me, I'm talking to you!'

Bruce was right up in Adam's face in a flash. And his manure-like breath was right up in Adam's nose too. Adam could not understand how, with all their millions of pounds, Bruce's super-rich family couldn't buy him a place at a posh school far, far away, or maybe just buy him some manners, or at least some *new breath*.

Head down. Don't react. He'll get bored soon and leave you alone. Adam repeated this mantra over and over in his head. He thought of Bruce as a vicious cat with its claws out, waiting to rip something to shreds. And he thought of himself as a ball of wool. Any response, anything at all, even eye contact, would be like shaking the wool right in front of Bruce's face, giving him the green light to attack.

'Where are your manners, Beales?! You're not even looking at me! I bet you'd look at me if I pretended to be your mum, eh? You gave *her* enough attention outside your baby brother's school, didn't you? Kissin' her goodbye like you're a wee baby too!'

And while they're out shopping for some new breath, surely Bruce's family could afford to buy him a new personality!

Head down. Don't react. He'll get bored soon and leave you alone.

'I almost threw up when I saw that! The most messed-up thing I've ever seen! I wouldn't kiss your mammy if you paid me! No wonder your dad decided to pop his clogs early! Nothing worth living for, know what I'm saying?'

Head! Down!

Adam's blood boiled.

Don't! React!

His jaw clenched.

He'll get bored soon and leave you alone!

It took all of Adam's strength not to lash out at Bruce. But Adam swallowed his rage. He bit down on his impulses and marched on.

'Oooooh! I think he's getting angry! Look at him, clenching his teeth!' Bruce cackled with laughter like a particularly odorous hyena. 'Come on, Adam, take a swing at me. *Pleeease*, I'm begging you, just try it.'

Head down. Don't react. He'll get bored soon and leave you alone.

Just when Adam thought he couldn't take it any longer, his mantra finally worked. Bruce did get bored, and he hung back as Adam marched into his form room for registration.

In that moment, an idea bubbled up and began to crystallise in Adam's mind. He knew what had to be done. It would take a dash of bravery, a pinch of guts and just a dollop of careful planning …

Ethan, Adam's best friend, had been about to launch into his usual machine-gun routine of endless questions about Adam's weekend, but he stopped when he saw the steely glare etched into Adam's face.

'Whoa! *WHAT* is *UP* with *YOU?*' Ethan enquired, stepping forward to take a closer inspection of Adam's expression. 'You look like you just bit the head off a *wasp*! I mean you look *ANGRY*! Are you, like, in a proper bad mood, or have you actually got toothache or something? Is it because I didn't come round yesterday? Sorry, but, you know, my mum was making me clean my room *AGAIN*, and do my chores AGAIN, which I didn't do *AGAIN*, so she grounded me *AGAIN*. Is that why you're mad? Don't be mad … are you mad? We should call you Mad Adam. Or is it the smell? The corridors smell pretty rank again, right? Like they've been cleaned with a mop that's been dipped in old meat then sprinkled with warm cheddar. Right? Or is "Angry Adam" a better nickname? Adam-angry. Adam-gry. Or has your mum banned you from watching YouTube again? Or maybe Adam-Mad. Or Madadam … Madam!'

Ethan only spoke at one speed – one million miles per hour – and he decided that now might be a good time to take a breather.

'It's nothing,' said Adam, shrugging his backpack off his shoulders and opening the YouTube app on his phone. 'Best mood I've been in all year, as a matter of fact.'

His idea was becoming clearer now. The very thought of it began to excite him. His tiny triumph over Bruce ... the thing Callum had said about him being better than Ed Almighty ... his determination never to let Callum find out how uncool he really was ... together these thoughts had combined in Adam's head to concoct a truly explosive idea.

'The best mood you've been in all year? Really? Because someone needs to tell the face. I mean, that was some top-level bitterness back there. Or are you being sarcastic? *Were* you being sarcastic? Sarcasm-Adam. Sarcadam. You were being sarcastic, right? I can never tell with you!'

'No, seriously, I'm on top of the world right now,' Adam calmly assured him, all traces of his Bruce-induced fury evaporated as he searched through the YouTube app and clicked 'add account'.

'Oh,' said Ethan, surprised. 'Well ... like ... *why*?'

'Because tomorrow I'm going to create my first actual piece of YouTube content, and I know exactly what it's going to be.'

'Wait! What!?!' Ethan's pitch shifted, a small ball of half-chewed gum falling out of his gaping mouth. 'Is that what you're doing *now*? Right now? On your phone? You're doing it? You're finally, at long last, actually taking the one giant leap towards your lifelong dream? You're ... you're ... you're creating *your own channel*?'

Adam looked Ethan in the eye, and there, where the black void of anger had been, was now a twinkle of chilled cunning, a sparkle of slyness, and more than a glint of revenge.

3

The Plan

The rest of the day had been a BAD one for being bullied. Bruce had continued his tormenting over first break, and also over last break, and between those breaks he'd managed to squeeze in a spot of bullying over lunchtime too, when he had, one by one, taken every chip from Adam's plate and thrown them into the bin.

Usually an episode like this would put 'happy Adam' out of the picture for the entire evening. Instead of performing one of his renditions of 'When's Dinner?' or 'I'm Hungry' while dancing around his mum in the kitchen, he would shut himself away in his bedroom and attempt to drown out his thoughts by playing loud music, or by turning off all the lights and trying to force himself to go to sleep, just so his brain didn't have to replay all the horrible moments of his day.

But this day was different – Adam *had* shut himself away in his room after school, but not because he was feeling sad, because he was the *opposite* of that – he was a frenzy of buzzing energy, making notes, packing bags, messaging Ethan and preparing himself for the day that would begin his career as a YouTuber.

Adam was just in the middle of cleaning up his PC's hard drive so that it would behave itself when it came to editing and uploading tomorrow's video, when there was a knock at his door, and Callum poked his little head in (actually, for the sake of accuracy, it was quite a large, round head, but it was on a little body).

He paused to take in the scene – music blaring, papers everywhere, string and wire all over the rug, an old David Attenborough nature programme on the TV, and something that looked like weird, radioactive hair gel dribbling off the edge of Adam's desk – then he finally spoke up.

'Are you ready to do my interview yet, Adam?' He used his extra-special polite voice, the one he only ever unleashed when he needed someone to help him with his homework.

'Yes. Soon. Sorry. Bit busy right now, but I'll be there in a minute, I promise, Cal.' Adam used his extra-special apologetic voice, the one he unleashed whenever he'd promised to help Callum with something, then completely forgotten about it.

'OK, cool, well, I'll be in my room, when you're ready.'

'OK, be there soon. Sorry. Again.'

'I can help, if you like? Maybe you might finish quicker if I do. What are you doing anyway?' he said, wandering into the room and gazing at the chaos.

'Sorry, Cal, it's kind of a one-man job. I'll be with you soon though. Promise.'

But Callum didn't take the hint. In fact, Callum didn't even appear to have heard. Something had distracted him. He'd come to hover behind Adam's shoulder, and he was staring at the open folder of videos on the computer screen.

Adam knew Callum was staring at one file in particular – one of their favourite videos of Dad. They'd watched it over and over again – 'First Day of Secondary School'. Mum had filmed it over a year ago, as Adam had been heading out of the door for day one at his new school and Dad was offloading non-stop advice.

Adam knew that Callum had memorised every word. 'Don't forget,' Dad began, 'your classmates will be feeling just as nervous as you, so be as friendly as you can. To *everyone*. Look out for them, the same way you'd like someone to look out for you. And just enjoy it, OK? You're going to love it! Mostly. Not all of it. Some of it'll suck.' And then he finished it all off with a mega Dad-hug and his favourite phrase – 'Love you *one million.*'

It was just a cheesy line that Dad had stolen from a superhero film, but Adam knew how much Callum missed Dad saying it to them.

He could tell that Callum was about to ask if he could watch the video of Dad again, but Adam did not have time for that.

'Hey! Callum! Earth to Callum! I'll come

24

through to you as soon as I'm done, OK? But right now I need some space.'

'OK. Sorry. How long? Roughly?'

'Ten minutes,' Adam replied distractedly. 'Fifteen tops.'

'OK. Thanks, Adam.'

So Callum quietly backed out of the room, and Adam continued his frantic preparations while quietly feeling bad that next year, when Callum would be starting secondary school, he wouldn't get to hear Dad's advice for himself.

Twenty minutes later, Callum's oversized head peeked back in through the doorway.

'Nearly done?'

'Two minutes. I promise!'

Ten minutes after that.

'Ready yet?'

'Allllll ... most. Sorry, bud. Not long.'

Twenty-three minutes after that, Adam's forehead was resting on his desk, with his bulging backpack next to him, when his bedroom door quietly squeaked open one last time.

'Adam, it's been aaaaages ...' Callum stopped

there as Adam interrupted him with a deafening snore.

Callum's face dropped.

'OK. Never mind,' he whispered. 'Night, Adam. Can't wait to find out what you've been planning. Knowing you, it's going to be the coolest thing ever.'

And out he went, leaving Adam to sleep at his desk alongside his backpack, which was overflowing with the strangest array of odds and ends – a reel of Dad's old fishing wire, a pair of scissors, some gaffer tape, a big tub of slime and even Adam's radio-controlled car that he hadn't played with in years. But weirdest of all was the purple papier-mâché octopus that Adam had made the previous summer, and which had been hanging from the ceiling of the school's art room until earlier that day …

Callum had got one thing right – it really was going to be the coolest thing ever.

4

The Coolest Thing Ever
(sort of)

'OK, so off you go-go!' said Jamie, with a clap of his hands. Jamie was actually called Mr Parkin, but he told all his art students to call him Jamie because, according to him, 'When it comes to art, being formal will only hold you back.' Jamie had said this when Adam had first started at the school, and he had never forgotten it.

What Adam *had* forgotten though was every single word Jamie had said right before the words 'OK, so off you go-go.' Adam was way too preoccupied with talking to Ethan's bag. Or, to be precise, he was talking to Ethan's phone, which was poking out of a pocket of the bag. Or, to be *even more* precise,

27

he was talking to the *MILLIONS OF YOUTUBE VIEWERS WHO WERE WATCHING HIM LIVE-STREAM ON TO HIS CHANNEL!*

(OK, so maybe it wasn't exactly 'millions' of viewers. It was actually a little closer to 'one' viewer. OK, it was *exactly* one viewer. And, well ... that one viewer might actually have been Ethan, who was watching it on Adam's phone, just to make sure it was working properly.) Yes, Adam had logged in to his brand spanking new YouTube account on Ethan's phone – better camera, better audio, less likely to crash mid-stream – and he was broadcasting live at that very moment.

'I don't want to ruin the surprise and give too much away,' Adam was whispering to Ethan's camera in a very 'David-Attenborough-surrounded-by-dangerous-animals' kind of way while the rest of his art class buzzed with activity, completely unaware that something extremely out of the ordinary was going on in the pocket of Ethan's bag. 'But I think you'll find everything you need to know in the title of this live stream. So hold on to your seats. Because this ... is going to be ... *epic*.'

The title of the live stream was 'Revenge on School Bully'. And Adam was not wrong – it really was going to be epic!

'So there are three things you need to know about this video,' Adam continued to camera. 'One – I have been at school since stupid o'clock so I could set everything up without anyone seeing. Two – you do not need to worry, the person at the receiving end of this prank deserves *everything* coming to him. And three – you should *not* try this at home. OK, here goes …'

Adam turned to check the back of the room. There was Bruce, exactly where they needed him to be, laying a large sheet of brown paper over his desk. Then, fleetingly, Adam shifted his glance one metre above Bruce's head. There, back in its usual spot, dangling from the ceiling, was the bright purple octopus. Even Adam could barely see the thin black line in its underbelly where he had sliced it open. There was no way anyone could have guessed that he had kitted it out with a dozen modifications, least of all the great big idiot sitting directly under it.

Ethan handed Adam his phone back, and Adam launched the app for his radio-controlled car – 'RC-99' – and let his thumb hover over the app's virtual control stick.

Bruce was chuckling, showing his friends what he had drawn – *Probably something childish and rude*, thought Adam. And then Adam heard the voice-over from last night's nature documentary playing out in his head.

The alpha male is unaware of his challenger's ambush. He has reigned supreme as the king of his pack for so many years he has become complacent and lazy.

Bruce wrapped the sheet of paper around his waist and mimicked a hula dance, making his gang of hangers-on chuckle and splutter.

Adam shuffled closer.

The challenger closes in on his target – unseen and unheard.

Adam pressed his thumb down on the screen of his phone …

He launches his attack.

Up inside the purple octopus, the RC motor whirred to life, the wheels spun, reeling in the fishing wire, the fishing wire pulled on a hinge, the 'doors' in the octopus's stomach snapped open. The tub of slime began to tip towards the opening, and then …

The doors snapped shut again.

The challenger falters, afraid his scent has been carried in on the breeze …

Adam looked at Bruce, worried he might have heard the whining motor, but Bruce was still oblivious to the mechanical storm brewing above his head. Adam looked up at the octopus and pressed his thumb down again. Nothing. He pulled the controls back, then forwards again. Still nothing.

The challenger resumes his attack.

Adam guessed he must have been out of range, so, in the pretence of gathering his art supplies, he moved a little closer to Bruce.

No slime storm.

He moved closer still.

Nothing.

And again.

Still no slime!

He was now only one desk away from Bruce, and then …

'Sir, I mean, Jamie! Adam Beales is trying to take

photos of my butt with his great-great-great-grandad's phone!' bellowed Bruce, snatching the phone from Adam's hand.

The entire class erupted in laughter, all except for Adam and Ethan.

'Can I have it back, please,' said Adam, in a way that was more of an order than a question.

'Wait, what even *is* this?'

Bruce scowled at Adam's screen, inspecting the RC-99 controls.

'Give. It. Back,' growled Adam.

'Are you playing *games* in *lesson time*?' gasped Bruce, as dramatic as if he were in a pantomime.

The entire class was watching as, almost as though it were happening in slow motion, Bruce pressed down on the controls …

Adam reached to snatch it away from him …

The purple octopus opened up …

Adam and Bruce wrestled over the phone …

The tub of slime tipped all the way over, and out fell its contents …

Down …

Down …

Down …

All over Adam's head.

The laughter was deafening.

Ethan snatched his phone from the pocket of the bag and ended the live stream before Adam could make any more of a fool of himself, *live on YouTube*.

But it was too late.

The damage was done.

The ambush was unsuccessful. The alpha male reigns supreme. His challenger is humiliated, tail tucked firmly between his legs.

'No way!' Bruce howled with laughter as Adam desperately tried to clean his face with his sleeves. 'No *way*! Beales, was that meant for *me*? Were you actually trying to prank *me*? Ohhhh, Beales, you are so going to pay for that.'

And then Adam, with slime in his eyes, heard the three worst sounds he had ever heard in his life:

1. The sound of his phone hitting the floor.
2. The sound of Bruce's foot crunching down on his screen.

3. The sound of Bruce, growling quietly in Adam's ear – 'You better watch your back, Slimeboy, cos I'm gonna make you wish you were never born. Know what I'm saying? You mess with the Bruce, you get the juice.' (Adam had no idea what to 'get the juice' was supposed to mean. He had a feeling Bruce had

no idea either, and he'd just said it because it rhymed with Bruce, and he thought it somehow sounded menacing. But Adam did know what 'make you wish you were never born' meant, so that's the bit he really focused on here, and he came to the conclusion that, in general, this was pretty bad news.)

5

The Surprise

From that moment on, Adam's bad luck seemed to spread through everything around him, like a leaky bottle of Coke in a bag full of schoolbooks. The first place his bad luck dribbled was directly through his YouTube account, where his unfortunate live stream had been autosaved to his channel, leaving it on full view for anyone to watch as many times as they wanted (or until they puked from laughing so hard). The bad luck then trickled through the rumour mill, and dripped through every classroom in school until there wasn't a single pupil in the building who hadn't watched it. At least twelve times. And then shared it with everyone they had ever met. But it wasn't until Adam stepped out from his final lesson of the day, dressed in his PE kit, with his slimy clothes stuffed in his bag, that he realised just how far his bad luck had spread.

It had flooded the entire corridor. People had raced from their classrooms just to get a glimpse of their school's new celebrity – Slimeboy, the stupidest kid who ever lived – taking his walk of shame through the school's main hallway. Adam could barely move for the mass of bodies that had gathered to laugh and point and jeer. No matter how fast he tried to get out of there, it was not fast enough.

Soon the cheering turned into a chant, and finally the chant grew to a deafening chorus as one word was bellowed over and over and over –

'*SLIMEBOY! SLIMEBOY! SLIMEBOY! SLIMEBOY!*'

Back at home, Adam was starting to feel a tiny bit better. Once he'd finally made it outside of school, he'd decided that getting on a bus full of chanting idiots wouldn't be much fun. So he'd walked home. Very quickly. So quickly, in fact, that even his torrent of bad luck struggled to keep up. Adam was happy to confirm that not a single person had followed him, and he hadn't heard a single whisper of 'Slimeboy' echoing out behind him since.

He'd even managed to evade both Mum and Callum upon entering the house, and by 6 p.m. he'd also managed to get all remnants of green slime from his school uniform, even if it had taken dabbing and cleaning with damp cloths for about one billion hours.

He was just beginning to hope that he could forget the word 'Slimeboy' for the rest of the night, when, suddenly –

KNOCK! KNOCK!

Someone's at the door, on a Tuesday night? thought Adam.

'Adam, can you get that, please?' Mum shouted from a bathroom full of steam and bubbles.

'No, we don't want a subscription to your thingy-me-bob. No, we don't want our gutters cleaned. Yes, we do have a TV licence.' Adam was practising a variety of possible responses while taking the stairs two at a time.

He pulled the door open, and the word NO was just about to slip out when––

'Hello, Adam, is it?'

Framed in the doorway was a smartly dressed man who spoke with authority. An equally well-dressed woman stood by his side, a weirdly strained smile on her face. Adam didn't recognise either of them, or the fancy car with tinted windows parked outside.

'All right, Bea – um, Adam.'

Adam might not have recognised the man and the woman, but he would have known that voice anywhere. His heart sank as Bruce emerged sheepishly from the car, carrying a small white box.

What the Jeff … was the only sentence that filled Adam's brain.

'I'm Stan, and this is Steph,' the large, well-dressed man carried on. 'We're Bruce's parents. Forgive me, this is all rather embarrassing, but it's come to our attention that *our son* damaged your property today at school. A mobile phone, I believe, yes?' He darted a look of disdain towards Bruce.

'Um, well, ahhh …' Adam struggled to understand what was happening.

'Listen, we'd like to keep this between us, as I'm

sure you'll appreciate,' Bruce's mum said, her weird smile getting weirder by the second. 'Bruce understands and accepts that what he did was wrong and has come to offer this by way of an apology.' She put a hand on Bruce's shoulder and nudged him closer to the doorstep. '*Haven't you*, Brucey?'

'Brucey' looked like nothing could be further from the truth, but to Adam's amazement he managed to force a very quiet 'sorry' from between his teeth. It looked like it hurt. 'Here,' Bruce went on, pushing the white box into Adam's still-very-confused arms

and then shoving his hands in his pockets with a shrug of his shoulders. 'Have this instead. I've got another at home anyway.'

Out of the box Adam pulled what looked like a brand-new iPhone, its flawless screen glistening in the porch light.

OK, who is this guy and what has he done with Bruce? Adam thought.

'Wonderful!' Steph said. 'We'll call this matter closed then, and I trust we'll have no further issues.'

Before Adam could reply, Stan and Steph were marching back down the path without a second glance. Bruce made as if to follow them, but turned back at the last second with a strange smirk on his face.

'You might have got a better phone out of this,' he whispered, 'but nobody's going to be forgetting the name Slimeboy any time soon. What is it now – over a million views and counting?'

Adam waited until Bruce had disappeared behind the tinted windows of the Kilters' ridiculously large car, and then pushed the door closed. He leaned against it in a flabbergasted state of shock.

He turned the phone on, expecting it to be completely broken, but it wasn't – *it worked*.

'Who was it?' said his mum as she emerged from the bathroom with a towel wrapped around her head.

'It was, er, someone from school. Bruce Kilter. And his mum and dad,' Adam muttered in a dreamlike state as he drifted upstairs, eyes glued to his new phone. 'Came to give me this.'

'*Stanley and Stephanie?* Gave you a *phone?* Who was it really?'

'Bruce stamped on my old one, so they, er… brand new… iPhone.'

'The Kilters actually *gave* you that? Well, they must have changed a lot since Stanley worked for your dad, is all I can think.'

If Adam had been listening properly, he might have wondered why his mum, who usually had a kind word about everyone, was being quite so sniffy about Bruce's parents. But his brain was too fixated on those final words Bruce had said to notice his mum's furrowed brow.

A million views and counting – it couldn't be true.

Please don't let it be true!

'It's not like them to give things away.' Mum was puzzling over the free phone. 'Perhaps their hearts are in the right place after all. I hope you said a *very* big "Thank You"!'

'Slimeboy ...' Adam drifted past. 'One million views ...'

'Adam, have you been listening to a single word I've said?'

'Wha–? Oh. Yeah. OK. I'll tidy it up later.' Then he disappeared into his bedroom and kicked the door shut behind him.

Adam's heart was pounding with fear.

Has my video gone viral?

He had always dreamed of going viral, but not like *this*. Not as *Slimeboy*!

My video's gone viral??

His trembling fingers logged in to his YouTube account. That worked too!

He waited for the page to load.

It had to be a lie, it couldn't be true –

My video ... has gone ... viral???

The page loaded, he found his 'Revenge on School

Bully' video, and then Adam's head silently exploded, his new phone dropped on to his bed, and his room was filled with five terror-filled words –

'MY VIDEO HAS GONE VIIIIIIIRRRRRRR-AAAAAAALLLLLLLL!!!!!!!'

Once again, Adam spent all evening shut away in his room. This time he wasn't *planning* a YouTube video, he was *watching* one. And he, Adam, was the hapless star of the show.

The video had a staggering one point eight million views! One point eight million people had watched him make a complete fool of himself. It was humiliating beyond belief. It was cringe-inducing beyond comprehension. It was 'oh-my-life-I-wish-I'd-never-been-born'-ish-ness beyond all reasonable sense. To put it simply, Adam was finally the star of a banger, and it was the worst day of … it was the *second* worst day of his life. A full, unrelenting, eight-minute video of him carefully prepping the prank, clumsily triggering the purple octopus, then, like the biggest idiot in the history of the internet, standing directly under his own trap, and taking a bucketload of slime to the face.

Adam stared at his monitor with blank, emotionless disbelief for a full ten minutes after the video finished. His dad smiled up at him from the framed black-and-white photo on his desk. It was a smile that usually seemed full of warmth and reassurance for Adam, but today it felt more like it was mocking him. All he wanted to do was run away and hide.

Then, almost as though the world was rubbing it in his face, a hinge gave way in his anglepoise lamp, causing the lamp to suddenly swivel and literally shine a spotlight on him, while downstairs his mum flicked the radio on to a song which blared out the lyrics – *Nowhere to run, nowhere to hide, nowhere to run to, baby!*

Adam decided that maybe this was a sign. What if he didn't try to hide from this video? What if he *embraced* it? What if the Slimeboy nickname didn't have to be a curse? What if it became a *blessing*?

In an instant he'd changed his channel name –

'"Slimeboy Adam". Take that, YouTube, do your worst!' He leaned back in his seat and smiled at the possibility. *If I can't beat 'em, I might as well join 'em.*

Sure, this was definitely not the YouTube notoriety he had been dreaming of, and yes, he had been made a massive fool of on an international platform, but at least people had *noticed* him. *And as long as people are watching me*, thought Adam, *and as long as I've got this fancy new phone with a working camera, I may as well give them SOMETHING ELSE to watch!*

That 'something else' needed to be really special. It had to grab people's attention. It had to be bigger and better than this prank-fail video. And Adam had absolutely no idea what it was going to be.

'How do you make it big on YouTube?' he asked Google.

Google didn't give him any quick answers.

'How do I get popular online?'

Still no good.

'How do I win on the internet?'

And this time something truly amazing appeared on his screen …

'Oh!' Adam gasped. 'Oh, wow!' He could hardly believe what he was looking at. 'This … this has to be … the *worst* pop-up ad I've ever seen in my life!'

Just like every other bit of tech in Adam's house, his computer was old, out of date and barely worked. This meant suffering pop-up ads *all the time*. This particular pop-up ad was so bad it was good – bright red writing, on a bright blue background – it looked like it had time-travelled directly from the 1990s.

Want to Win the Internet? Click HERE to find out how!

It was clearly a simple algorithm that created an instant (and very fake) advert for whatever you had just searched for. Adam could not stop laughing at its lameness.

'Or, how's about I click riiiight *here* instead?!' he chuckled as he sent his cursor to the X in the top right-hand corner.

The ad disappeared, then immediately returned, but this time it read –

Want to be an awesome dude? You're just one CLICK away!

'"Awesome dude?"' snorted Adam. 'I don't think so. Goodbye!'

X

The box vanished.

And then it came back.

Cool boys click this LINK!

X

Find out how to be part of the popular crew, HERE!

X

Want to be snazzy?

X

You too can be a trendy homie!

X

Fancy pants!

X

The cat's pyjamas!

X

X

X

'Oh my life! Take the hint! GO! (X) A! (X) WAY!'

X

X! X! X! X! X! X! XXXXXXXXXXXX!!!

Finally the advert relented and Adam was, at last, able to continue scrolling the search page. Until …

Adam! PLEASE! Would you just click the stupid link?

Adam froze, staring at the advert in disbelief.

'Ohhh-kayyy. Well, that was weird.'

Sorry, Adam. Didn't mean to freak you out. But, seriously, if you would just click through. I promise you won't regret it.

'What the … Who's doing this?'

My name is Popularis Incrementum, and I am an AI that will solve all your problems. Trust me.

'Whoa,' whispered Adam.

Just then there was a knock at the door and Callum poked his head in.

'Adam? Do you think you can help me with my school project tonight? Can we use the new phone?'

'Err, not now, Callum, I'm ...' *Freaking out because my computer's talking to me.* '... busy,' Adam gabbled, pushing his door closed again.

'How are you even answering me?' he muttered at his monitor. 'I mean, there's not even a mic!'

I can't hear you. My name is Popularis Incrementum. I am a computer program. I use artificial intelligence to predict what your next question will be.

'Whoa! So, you can, like, *read my mind*?!'

No. As I believe I already explained. My name is Popularis Incrementum. I am a computer program. I use artificial intelligence to predict what your next question will be. And I am right 98.6 per cent of the time.

'All right then, what colour am I thinking of?'

Banana.

'Ha!'

Or blue. That question is nearly always a fruit or a colour.

'Oh. Well … wow. What are tomorrow's lottery numbers going to be?'

My name is Popularis Incrementum. I am a computer program. I use artificial intelligence to predict what your next question will be. I can't predict the future.

'What the … Are you *sure* you can't hear me?!'

Yes. I am sure.

'OK then, how many fingers am I holding up?'

Try asking something impossible for me to know the answer to. "How many fingers" is a textbook question and would only prove whether or not I can see you, not hear you.

'Man, this is getting really weird. OK, try this – my best friend, Ethan, on his seventh birthday, what shape was his birthday cake?'

Popularis Incrementum said nothing. The cursor just sat there, blinking, like it was waiting for someone to reply to a text. Or like it was *thinking*. And then, finally, it replied.

That is impossible for me to know the answer to.

'Yes! So, wait … No, that only proves you were right. OK, let me try to figure this out …'

My name is Popularis Incrementum. I am a VERY BUSY computer program. I don't have all day. Either click, or don't.

A countdown began in the bottom corner of the ad – *10 ... 9 ... 8 ...*

The reverse psychology worked. Adam was intrigued.

KNOCK! KNOCK!

Callum again. 'When do you think you'll be ready, only ... ?'

'Callum! Not now!'

Adam pushed the door closed again.

7 ... 6 ... 5 ...

His mouse hovered over the link.

KNOCK! KNOCK!

'Adam, can you just ... ?'

'NO, CALLUM! GET LOST!'

He kicked the door shut.

4 ... 3 ... 2 ...

No. Don't click. It would be a stupid thing to do.

He let go of his mouse.

1

CLICK!

Against all his instincts, Adam's curiosity got the better of him. Or, at least, it got the better of his cursor finger.

Congratulations on finally making a decision. I shall go now. But I won't be leaving you.

'Huh? You're going, but you're not *leav*...' Adam trailed off, mid-sentence, because just then the advert vanished and a new page appeared. It looked so like a *real* page, made of actual paper – gold and shimmering in a way that didn't seem possible – that Adam had to reach out and touch his screen just to check. And as he did, black text began to scrawl across it, as if someone were writing it there and then.

Popularity now is your ultimate prize
So heed this advice, or meet your demise
Grow to one million by this time next year
Do it not, and lose all that you hold dear

Adam stared at it.

'What does it mean?' He was talking to his computer, but Popularis was not talking back.

'Popularis! I don't get it!' And then the page dissolved away, leaving his empty YouTube account staring back at him.

Adam recited the riddle over and over in his head, and then, slowly, it began to make sense. If it was a real riddle, meant just for him (which it obviously wasn't), then maybe it was telling him to 'get one million people to subscribe to your channel' or lose the channel completely (which it obviously wasn't).

But he barely had a moment to ponder this before—

BEEEEEEEEEEP!

His computer started squealing out a high-pitched, brain-piercing tone.

The screen began to glow a blinding white. Brighter ... brighter ... *brighter*! And then –

FLASH!

A jolt of electricity kicked him in the brain.

FLASH!

A deafening screech tore at his ears.

FLAAAAASSSSHHHH!

Adam opened his eyes. He was on the floor, next to his chair. The room was eerily silent. The computer screen was ominously black. Adam's heart was violently pounding. Panic was rapidly taking over. Had he just let a hacker in? Had he rolled a chair leg over an electrical cable and severed the wire?

Adam jumped back on to his chair and tried to power his computer up again. According to the green light next to the power button it was still on, but, according to the monitor, it was dead. He scribbled the mouse around on his desk. Nothing. He clicked the buttons. No response.

'Please don't let it be dead! Please don't let it be dead! Please don't let it be dead!' he pleaded to Rama-C-Drive, the god of computers, as he continued frantically clicking the mouse. But, in his heart of hearts, he realised it was futile. Not just because there was no such thing as Rama-C-Drive, the god of computers, but because, deep down, he knew that his computer would not be waking up again. And Adam's 'deep down-ometer' was never wrong.

And then his computer woke up again.

(His 'deep-down-ometer' was sometimes wrong.)

Adam watched with relief as light radiated back

into his screen. His YouTube account reappeared (with *no* pop-ups), and then he saw his cursor dance around as the computer began playing catch-up with all the scribbling and clicking he'd been doing while it had been taking a rest.

Scribble-click, scribble-click, scribble ...

Click – one of the hundreds of clicks landed on the 'Upload Video' button of his YouTube page.

Scribble-click, scribble-click, scribble ...

Click – 'Select Video'.

'No, no, no!' Adam gasped. 'What is going on here?! Stop it! STOP!'

With the most unbelievable sequence of bad luck, the random scribbles and clicks that Adam had performed thirty seconds earlier were now dancing around on his screen, almost of their own accord, and clicking through each and every step of the upload process on his YouTube page!

'No!' Adam pleaded, grabbing the mouse again and bashing every key on his keyboard. 'No! No! NO!'

There were videos on there that he definitely did *not* want to share with the world.

Scribble-click, scribble-click, scribble-click …

Adam pictured what his life would be like if anyone at school ever saw his 'Nappy-rena' video (basically Adam dancing around in his bedroom, wearing nothing except an oversized nappy and singing along to 'Macarena', only he changed the words to 'Nappy-rena'. It seemed like a good idea at the time). His panic hit overload. Beading sweat prickled his face … He watched helplessly while his computer clumsily progressed through one step after another. It selected a random video from his desktop. It clicked 'Next'. Adam pounded on the computer's power button, but it refused to respond. And then he saw it – the 'Publish' button …

'No, no! No, no, no! NO! NO! NOOO!'

He dived for the power cable, yanked it from the wall, stared up at the screen, and then …

Adam breathed a long sigh of relief. His computer had finally powered down.

He collapsed on his bed, struggling to believe just how bizarre all that weirdness had been. He knew there was no such thing as magic. He definitely knew there was no such thing as a Magical

Internet Pop-Up Ad! But all the same, how could you explain everything that just happened?

All he knew was that he was glad it was over.

Except it wasn't over. Not completely.

As he lay there on his bed, Adam would have freaked out if he'd spotted that instead of displaying the time – 22:10 – his alarm clock was showing the numbers 3:65. He would have freaked out even more if he'd realised that 365 was the exact number of days that Popularis had given him to 'Grow to one million by this time next *year*'. But the weirdest part of all, the thing that would have freaked Adam out beyond all reason, was that the clock wasn't even plugged in.

6

Fluffy News

'OK, take two.'

Adam woke up excited. Too excited to faff around resetting Bruce's phone. Too excited to care that, downstairs, Mum had the breakfast news on way too loud while he was trying to make a video. Too excited to care that it was impossible to set up the camera anywhere in his room that didn't make it look as though a herd of Trash Fairies had marched through it. And he was definitely too excited to get his head around everything that had happened the night before. All Adam knew was that he had a burning need to jump straight out of bed and make a video for YouTube as fast as humanly possible. He couldn't explain it. It was a desire so strong that it even overrode the urge to race down-stairs to check out why the house smelt like sugary waffles and pancakes.

Adam pushed all other thoughts, noises and smells to the other side of his brain, then pushed all his junk to the other side of his room as he plonked himself down in front of his camera.

'Good morning, YouTube!' he rehearsed as he switched his camera on and checked his hair. 'My name is Slimeboy Adam, and have I got BIG news for you!'

He psyched himself up, mentally preparing himself by jogging on the spot ...

'Yes!'

By inhaling and exhaling huge lungfuls of air ...

'Go!'

By slapping his cheeks ...

'Ouch!'

By laughing maniacally at his reflection ...

'Weird.'

By pretending to be attacked by Mr Snuffles (his toy cat) ...

'OK, stop now.'

He sat back down and put his serious face on.

'You're the cool Adam,' he reminded himself as he checked his position in the frame, 'not the school Adam. You're going to explain this new challenge that Popularis Incrementum gave you – except don't mention Popularis. Enthral them. Intrigue them. Can Adam complete the challenge on time? Will he fall flat on his face? People are going to be hooked. For a whole year! OK, let's do this! You are absolutely going to …'

'ADAAAAAMMM!' An ear-shredding scream erupted downstairs, sending chills of terror down Adam's spine. 'WHAT HAVE YOU DONE?!'

Adam had a niggling suspicion that this was not going to be good.

'Hey, what's up?' Adam squeaked as he nervously shuffled into the living room to find his mum glaring at the weatherman on TV.

'WHAT WERE YOU THINKING?!' she barked, whipping her head round to focus her death-stare on him.

'*What?*'

'What do you *mean* "what"? I'll show you *WHAT*!'

She skipped the live TV back. Back before the weather, back to the news presenters on the morning breakfast show, back to the final news segment of the day – the Fluffy News. 'Fluffy News' was what Adam's mum called the nice, happy, fun little bit that they always showed towards the end of the show – usually some home footage of a singing dog, or a kitten that had made friends with a crocodile, or a baby that giggled uncontrollably at a piece of toast.

Is this some overly dramatic way of telling me I'm late? Adam wondered to himself. They were supposed to be out of the door and on the way to school by the time the Fluffy News started. But this was far, *far* worse than that.

Adam's mum pressed play, and the Fluffy News began again.

'*And if this next clip hasn't popped up on your social media rounds so far this morning, we can guarantee it's only a matter of time,*' said one of the hosts.

'*Err, yes, and if the young lads in the video haven't been grounded yet, I can guarantee* that's *only a matter of time too!'* added the other. *'Take a look at this prank that produces hair-raising results …'*

Adam's eyes almost popped out of their sockets at what he was seeing.

He fell to his knees.

Clasped his hands over his mouth.

There, on national TV, was his bathroom door. And when that bathroom door opened, there was his mum's furious face. And on top of his mum's furious face was a shock of sticky, slimy, bubbly, gluey hair, reaching up so high it almost touched the ceiling. And then the image began to shake as, off

camera, Adam and Callum began laughing their heads off.

Adam could barely breathe. How could this have happened? His 'Glue Shampoo' video had just been shown on the breakfast news! But most shocking of all, for Adam at least, was the credit at the bottom of the screen — 'Slimeboy Adam YT'. The video was from his very own YouTube channel.

Adam's entire world was spinning in disbelief.

It had happened.

Despite unplugging his PC, last night's accidental upload *had* completed!

One single, random video had zipped out of his computer, straight on to YouTube, and then someone at breakfast news thought it was a good idea to beam it on to millions of TV screens across the UK!

This was awful!

This was *awesome*!

He was practically *famous*!

And then a pang of guilt tugged at Adam's conscience because, deep down inside, he was cheering with relief that it was his mum and her gluey hair being paraded on national TV, and not *him* dancing the 'Nappy-rena'.

Adam looked down at his phone and saw that, since his YouTube channel was linked to all his other online accounts, his social media had gone through the roof – Twitter, TikTok, Instagram …

'Mum …' he gasped in amazement, 'you're an international *superstar*!'

Adam couldn't contain a whoop of laughter as he turned his phone around to show the others.

'What?!' Callum squealed in amazement. 'No WAY!'

Even their mum had to let out a laugh when she saw the number of views the video had so far.

'Eight *MILLION*?!' she screamed. 'Adam! Eight million people have seen me looking like *that*?!'

Adam could not believe it. Somehow, *he*, Adam Nobody Beales, had trended, not just once, but *two days in a row*! His dreams of becoming a YouTuber were finally coming true, and he couldn't help feeling that Popularis Incrementum was the reason why.

7

Looking Up

'Hey, guys, it's Slimeboy Adam here! Wow! Thank you so much for supporting my first video so ... so ... I don't know, so *amazingly*.' Adam was buzzing way too much to do this video sitting at his desk, so he had taken his mum's phone cradle from her car, taped it to the handlebars of his bike and stuck his phone in it so that he could film himself talking to camera while he zoomed towards the park.

'I cannot believe the response!' he continued, the breeze blowing his hair back as he pedalled with effortless speed. 'And if you want more videos like that, then please click "Subscribe", because there is plenty more where that came from. In fact, I'm going to make sure of it, because yesterday's video kicked off something really big for me, and that's what brings me to the first of two surprises I've got lined up for you today. I'm going to introduce you to a little something I like to call – *SLIMEBOY ADAM'S ULTIMATE CHALLENGE!* Oh yes, it's not just any old challenge, it's the *ultimate* challenge! And this is where you all ask "*What could this extremely exciting ultimate challenge be?*" And *this* would be the moment where I say … *drum roll, pleeeeaaaaase!* SLIMEBOY ADAM'S ULTIMATE CHALLENGE IIIIISSSSSS … *TO GET ONE MILLION SUBSCRIBERS IN ONE YEAR!* Yes, you heard that correctly. If my maths is right, and it usually isn't, I need to get another nine hundred and ninety thousand subscribers in three hundred and sixty-four days. So … yeah, watch this space!'

'This space' was suddenly full of sky and trees, but no Adam as he quickly ducked out of the frame and screamed 'PIGEON!'

'Sorry, guys! Almost got decapitated by a low-flying pigeon there. Can you imagine? Death by pigeon! What a way to go!'

The video was going better than he could ever have hoped. He was managing to be 'cool' Adam rather than 'school' Adam (well, if you ignore the whole pigeon thing), and he had remembered to mention everything on his list of things to say. He was just finishing off, explaining how he had a huge library of ready-made videos lined up and itching to be uploaded, when he brought his bike to a standstill.

'OK, I'm at the park, and that brings me to the second of your two surprises – I'm going to perform a *trick*.' He flipped the camera so that it faced forwards, filming what Adam was seeing, rather than pointing upwards at his cold, pink face. 'That huge mound of earth over there, or that "hill", as some people might call it, is the best ramp in all of Northern Ireland. And that white ribbon stretched between the two trees on top of the hill – that is *exactly* one hundred and seventy-seven centimetres high, which is *exactly* the same height as me, and that is *exactly* what I'm going to jump over on this bike, while trying to count *exactly* how many times I said the word "*exactly*" in this sentence. And I'm going to perform this trick at exactly ... *now!*'

The bike rolled into action. The camera, filming everything Adam was seeing, began rocking from side to side as he pedalled frantically towards the grassy slope that separated the football field from the playground. 'It's been *years* since I've done this!' he panted as the bike sped closer and closer towards the hill. 'And I've never measured how high I can actually get. So I'm just hoping it'll work! And that I can still land it! Oh my life ... I can't believe I'm actually doing this! Here ... we ... GOOOOOO!'

Adam whooped as the bike rocketed up the slope, filling the screen with bright green grass zooming below him, then, as he shot into the air, the camera filmed nothing but cloudy October sky as Adam flew up, higher and higher. And then, as the bike descended and he brought the front wheels down, the screen was filled with – *the churning, spinning, grinding blades of the tractor-mower that was directly below him!*

Adam let out a scream of terror. The bike plummeted towards the whirring cylinders. He was about to be churned into a pulp and there was nothing he could do to stop it! He was falling too fast! The mower was too close! The driver couldn't see him!

Down ...

    Down ...

        Down he went and then ...

FLASH!

A jolt of electricity kicked him in the brain.

    FLASH!

A deafening screech tore at his ears.

        FLAAAAASSHHHHH!

Instead of Adam's *life* flashing before his eyes, it was his *phone screen*. And instead of dropping directly into the churning mower blades, he ... *dangled* there. In mid-air! For an entire second! Maybe *two*. Floating! As though he had been put on pause. Adam's heart lurched against his ribs. His mind bounced against the walls of his skull. *What is going on!?*

Beneath him the mower carried on, until the roof of the driver's cab was directly under him, and then – *WHOOOMPH!* The bike plummeted down, slammed into the roof of the mower, shot off the other side, whizzed through the air, crashed over the top of the playground's slide, rocketed down its entire length, flew off the end of it, soared *between* the chains of a swing and landed in the centre of the see-saw just as Adam slammed on his brakes. He teetered there for a precarious moment or two as the seesaw held itself perfectly level, halfway between seeing and sawing, then, slowly, it began to tip forwards, and with precision control Adam rolled down the other side, hopped gracefully over the seat and handles, then skidded to a stop in front of a roundabout full of slack-jawed six-year-olds.

'Oh my life!' Adam panted in breathless disbelief

as he flipped the camera back up to film his face. 'Oh my *life*! Oh-my-life oh-my-life *oh-my-life*! Tell me I got that on camera!'

He had. Perfectly. And no matter how many times he rewatched it, he still could not believe it had actually happened. It was beyond unbelievable. It was *stupidly* impossible! It was the most brain-meltingly non-doable stunt Adam had ever seen in his life. In fact, it was *so* impossible that Adam only managed to be exhilarated for 4.8 seconds. After that, his exhilaration was overshadowed by the mild sense of being *MAJORLY FREAKED-OUT IN A MIND-BLOWINGLY MASSIVE WAY!*

Back in his bedroom, Adam's trembling fingers were tripping so desperately across the keys of his computer that he couldn't manage to spell a single word correctly.

Popru-

Polp-

Poplu-

Ploppur-

Despite his feeble finger fumblings, he somehow managed to cause a window to pop up on his computer screen, and Adam jumped back in surprise to see what it said –

An analysis of your erratic and childlike keystrokes has deduced that you may be trying to contact me. How may I be of assistance?

'Popularis!' Adam blurted. 'I just … In the park … my bike … I …'

I wasn't being serious, Popularis interrupted. **I can't hear you, remember? I am a computer program. But a series of algorithms suggests that**

you are highly likely to be enquiring as to whether or not I am interfering with the course of your life. Correct?

'Well, yeah, I suppose. But more specifically I wanted to know if …'

Are you still actually talking to me? Do you even understand English? I. Can't. Hear. You. Get it?

'OK, yeah, I get it. But I don't know how else to communicate with y—'

You're still doing it, aren't you?

Adam clenched his mouth shut and forced himself to not reply. Then, eventually, a tiny little squeak of an utterance left his lips – 'No!'

Liar.

'Whatever! What difference does it make?! You're supposed to guess what my questions will be, so why don't you just … ?'

Only this much can be told:
Now and then
I will assist
To help you reach your goal.

'OK. Right. Yes. Thank you. But "assist" *how*?' Adam demanded, his words stumbling out of his mouth as clumsily as when he had been typing them. 'Assisting like you're just giving me advice? Like, just words on a screen? Or like you're giving me a ... *helping hand*, like, *physically*, in *real life*, like ... Popularis, I'm pretty sure something made my bike *float*. Like, in the *air*! Like someone had pressed pause on me! Like ... I don't know ... *MAGIC*?!'

My name is Popularis Incrementum. I am a computer program. I use artificial intelligence to predict what your next question will be. And this is getting weird. I shall go now. But I won't be leaving you.

The next day, as Adam dropped Callum at school, then continued to his own, the weirdness of the bike stunt was still lingering in his mind, like a strange smell that wouldn't go away. But when he reached his school gates, he was met with a sight so spectacular that it blew every molecule of weirdness straight out of Adam's mind.

There, right outside the front entrance, was a

crowd of kids, about twelve of them, mostly from the year below, all waiting to greet Adam with a cheer.

'Your channel legit rocks!' one of them called to him.

'Your video was *genuinely* on the news! I *genuinely* saw it!' said a wide-eyed girl with a cornflake in her hair as she rushed up to meet him.

'So, like, are you famous now, or what?'

'Your video was dead funny! Your mum's hair was dead funny! It was just, like, dead funny!'

'That stunt was *AWESOME*!' a gangly, curly-haired kid squealed at him. 'The way you jumped over that mower! And then down the slide! And *through* the swing! And then the bit on the see-saw! It was, like, *whoa*!'

Adam couldn't help laughing. It was all too surreal.

'My MAAAAN!' shouted Ethan, suddenly coming up behind Adam and slinging an arm around his shoulders. 'THIS IS WILD! Did you plan that? The trick? You know, the tractor-mower and everything? You planned it all, didn't you! You knew he was going to be there! Or you didn't. You so did! Seriously impressive editing skills too! That dangling bit almost looked *real*. And where did you learn those BMX stunts? Have you been having lessons? Tell me! No, don't tell me. TELL ME! You know what, I don't even wanna know! I don't care! Because my best friend … is … FAMOUS!'

Adam had no response but to laugh. Ethan was practically beetroot from his ballistic rapid-fire question-fest.

As they made their way into school, the questions didn't stop coming, but, strangely, not a single person seemed to care about how he'd managed the 'floating in mid-air' bit.

Adam was dumbstruck; the most magical aspect of his video was proving to be the *least* interesting part! Nobody thought it was real! Soon Adam found himself wondering the same thing. Was it real? Or had his bike just got caught on something for a moment? Getting snagged on a branch definitely sounded more likely than being paused in mid-air by an internet advert. And all the rest — landing on the slide, jumping through the swing — it could have all just been a fluke!

Adam didn't have long to ponder this, though, because the warm reception didn't stop at the

school gates … There was no dodging shouts of 'LOSER!' as he walked through the doors, no trying to lie low, no ignoring anyone. His head actually got to experience the novelty of being *held high* as he entered the school. For the first time ever, people said 'hi' to him! All day long, people came up to congratulate him – some were absolute strangers, some were classmates who had never spoken to him before – and, best of all, there was neither sight nor smell of Bruce. The whole day left him with a glowing sensation inside.

'I suppose you're *never* going to have time to help me with my project now you've got all this YouTube stuff to do?' said Callum on their walk back home that afternoon.

'What are you *talking* about? Of course I'll help you, you little Bean Head! Tonight, OK? As soon as I've uploaded today's video.'

Seeing Callum's small-but-giant face light up, it crossed Adam's mind to tell his brother all about Popularis Incrementum. But the words stuck to the roof of his mouth. He had a feeling that if he told anyone he was communicating with an online advert he would sound like a total fool. And he didn't particularly want to sound like a total fool, not now he was starting to feel a tiny bit cool for the first time in his life. It wasn't worth the risk.

If Adam could just keep his popularity level up until Callum started at his school next year, then all of his fears about being exposed as a loser would be ancient history. The thought made him feel all warm and fuzzy inside.

It was a feeling that came to a shuddering halt as he and Callum rounded the corner on to their road and saw the police car parked outside the house.

8

The Mission

It hadn't even been a year since their last car was stolen. It was an *amazing* car. They'd called it the *Dadmobile*, and it had never broken down. Not once. Dad and one of his friends had built it out of bits of other vehicles – the body of a 1974 Austin Maxi, the engine of a VW Golf, the alloy wheels of a Mini Cooper ... Dad had even fitted it with a prototype for an in-car computer. He'd designed it himself and it was the first of its kind. It didn't just tell you where to go; it showed you where the nearest petrol station was, or if your tyres needed pumping up, or how long it had been since you last went for a wee.

That car had been the only part of Dad that Mum, Callum and Adam had had left. Then, last summer, they woke up one morning to find that it had gone. Vanished. Stolen. And now the exact same thing had happened to their 'new' car. Of all the cars on their street, why had someone chosen to steal Mum's second-hand, sixteen-year-old banger? Now they had nothing.

Adam was way too furious to sleep. And when he did manage it, he dreamed he was still awake, so it hardly even counted. He couldn't help asking all the 'why's and 'what-if's in his mind – *Why us again? What if it was the same person who stole the Dadmobile? What if they're targeting us on purpose? Haven't we been through enough? What if the police don't catch them? They didn't catch anyone after the Dadmobile was stolen. What if I have to catch them myself? What if I find out where they live and get a box full of hungry rats delivered to their house? What if I could do something, anything to undo that look of despair on Mum's face? What if ... what if ... What if the thief comes back for more?*

This thought jolted Adam fully awake. At least ... *was* it the thought that had woken him, or was it a noise? Had someone actually coughed downstairs, or had Adam just dreamed it? Slowly and silently, he sat up in his bed. *Call the police. Right. Now!* He slid his phone from under his pillow, only to find it was dead – the second time that day – for such a shiny phone, it didn't have much of a battery. His clock said it was 3:61. Wait, 3:61? That wasn't even a proper time, maybe it was –

And then he froze. This time it was unmistakeable – someone was definitely moving around downstairs! Footsteps in the hall – a door being pushed open – footsteps in the kitchen – a cupboard door creaking – another cupboard door – footsteps in the hall – footsteps on the stairs – footsteps coming *up* the stairs!

Adam's brain went into free-fall, desperately scrabbling for a plan.

Footsteps on the landing.

His eyes darted this way, then that. No way out!

Footsteps outside his room.

And then Adam heard it …

Very quietly … someone … began … brushing their teeth in the bathroom and humming the *Countdown* theme tune.

He sank back into his pillow, limp with relief.

Mum! You almost gave me a heart attack! Adam thought. *What are you doing up in the middle of the night, anyway?*

He heard the rumble of a car engine outside. The horn sounded once, quickly. Mum rushed down the stairs and Adam pulled back the curtain in time to see her hurrying out of the house, climbing into the car, then disappearing into the night.

Itching with curiosity, Adam dashed downstairs hoping to find some kind of answer to what was going on. The first clue came when he saw the clock on the microwave – 6:02. It wasn't quite as 'middle-of-the-night' as he'd thought. And then he spotted the second clue, on the table – a note from Mum:

Morning, sweeties! Had to leave a little earlier today. I might be back later than usual too. Pizzas in freezer. Films in the TV. Mrs O'Bannon says to phone if you need anything. Love ya! Mum xx

Adam spotted the array of bus and train timetables at the other end of the table, and felt a lurch of sadness in his chest as he realised that, because she had no car, his mum was having to spend nearly *four* hours, switching between taxis, trains and buses, just to get to work. That would be eight hours a day!

The anger he had felt towards whoever had stolen their car was suddenly overshadowed by a steely determination to help his mum out. He just couldn't figure out *how*. It had taken *weeks* just to save up the measly £12.20 he'd collected in the New Gearbox Fund, and now, since that box was in the car, even *that* had gone.

He racked his brains for ideas. Sell some of his stuff? Since everything but his phone was completely worthless, he estimated that the sale of all his worldly possessions would rake in a grand total of £1.32! Win the lottery? Too young to even buy a ticket.

He wondered if it would be worth writing to some of the YouTubers he followed. Ed Almighty did loads of nice things for people who needed help – paying for someone's surgery, replacing someone else's broken washing machine; once he'd even bought someone a *house*. Maybe Ed might take pity on them, donate them a new car, and maybe even feature them in a video! Just the other week Ed had given all the money he'd made from one of his prank videos to charity. Hang on ... Adam played that memory back in his head. Had Ed said that he'd 'made money' from a video? Did YouTubers get *paid*? Somehow it had never even occurred to him before! *But they must make money*, he thought, *or how else do they pay for all that stuff?*

And then it came to him. The email! YouTube had sent him a million emails in the past few days, and he'd opened a grand total of three. But there was something about the title of this particular unopened email that stuck in Adam's mind – '*Monetisation*.'

He raced to his computer. He searched his inbox. There it was!

'*Congratulations!*' the email read. '*Your channel "Slimeboy AdamYT" is now eligible for monetisation ...*'

All he had to do was fill in a form, click a few buttons and he would start getting paid to have adverts in his videos. It was the first time in his life that he had danced around the house at 7:08 a.m. in his pyjamas without it involving unwrapping an extremely impressive birthday present.

Adam immediately began hatching a plan.

If he was very clever with this, he would be able to help his mum after all.

9

Things Get Serious

'FUDGE!' screamed Callum as he shuffled, bleary-eyed, from his room. 'What in the *WHY* are you dancing outside my bedroom?!'

'Eat up, little dude!' chirped Adam, thrusting a bacon sandwich into Callum's hands. 'We've got work to do!'

'What are you talking about?'

Adam answered this question by taking Callum in his arms, dancing him round in circles and 'singing' – 'Geeeeeetttttt ... dressed! Get dressed! Get dressed, get dressed, get dressed! Get dreeeeeesssssssssed ... Quick quick quick quick quick!'

Callum was seemingly not in the mood for a song and dance routine. He broke away from the twirling, took the now somewhat squishy sandwich from Adam's hand and shuffled back into his bedroom. Two minutes later, he reappeared, wearing his school uniform and a scowl.

'It's only seven thirty!' he protested, through a mouthful of bacon and bread. 'We've got ages till school!'

'We're leaving early,' explained Adam. 'I'm making a new video on the way, and you're going to help me.'

Adam was a man on a mission. Well, he was a *young* man on a mission. OK, fine, he was a boy on a mission, but he was a *big* boy. Adam was a big boy on a mission, and ... it doesn't quite have the same ring to it, does it? He gathered all the props he would need for the video and stuffed them into his backpack.

Callum, on the other hand, just stood there, mouth agape.

'Me? You want *me* to help? I'm going to be in your video?! YESSSS!'

'I'm a big boy on a mission, Callum. Try to keep up, because nothing's going to stop me,' declared Adam as he threw his bag over his shoulder and marched out of the house.

'Nothing?' Callum called after him.

'Nothing!'

'Not even the fact that you're still in your PJs?'

Adam did an about-turn and marched back into the house in his T-shirt and boxers.

'Nothing except partial nudity and public humiliation is going to stop me.'

Once he was dressed, Adam's hard work paid off. By the time school started, he had *two* brand-new videos in the can:

1. 'Last to Leave the Roundabout' where he and Callum went to the park and competed to stay on the spinning roundabout the longest (Callum won. Adam almost puked).
2. 'Hiding in a Bin to Scare My Best Friend' where, well, the title speaks for itself really – Adam hid in a park bin (he made sure to empty it first, obviously), waited for Ethan to walk past, then jumped out and …

'MUMMMYYY!' Ethan screamed as he ran for his life, smacked straight into a tree and knelt on the

grass, clutching his face. 'I'm going to be sick! I'm going to be sick! I've never been so scared in my life!'

Adam and Callum were also going to be sick because they'd never *laughed* so hard in their lives.

Once he'd stopped hyperventilating, Ethan saw the funny side too.

'Look at the way my face just bounces off the tree!' He beamed with pride as they sat on a park bench and watched the video back. 'I'm a comedy genius! I'm going to be an internet *sensation*!

Nobody's looked so foolish since ... since Adam slimed himself in school!'

Adam knew Ethan was right – there was no way that video wasn't going to be a huge hit!

He really was a big boy on a mission.

Over the next few weeks, the thought of his mum struggling so much to get to work spurred Adam on to make a brand-new video every day, without fail. Sometimes with Callum's help, sometimes on his own, but always with a steadily increasing subscriber count ...

Nov. 7th – 'Hiding Fake Slugs in My Little Brother's Shoes!'

Views: 60k   Subscribers: 20k

Number of kids waiting outside school: 14

Number of times Marcus Kane asked Adam if he wanted to move out of the 'Geek Seats' at the front of the class and sit next to him on the row behind: 4

Nov. 18th – 'Statue Challenge! How Long Can I Stand Still in the Middle of a Busy Shopping Centre?'

Views: 81k   Subscribers: 63k

Number of kids waiting outside school: 19

Number of times Marcus Kane asked if Adam wanted to sit next to him on the second row: 0 (because Heather Robson and Norah Gleeson made room for Adam and Ethan to sit next to them on the third row!)

Nov. 26th – 'I Had to Be My Little Brother's Servant for the Whole Day!'

Views: 156k   Subscribers: 107k

Number of kids waiting outside school: 25+ (all pretending to be Callum's servants, which was so funny it made it into Adam's next video!)

Number of times Simon Chan asked Adam if he wanted to sit next to him on the fourth row: 1 (It turned out Norah Gleeson was a lot more interested in talking about her pet snail farm than Adam really looked for in a close mate, so he jumped at the chance to move. He felt bad about leaving Ethan on the third row, but Adam was directly behind him, so it wasn't the end of the world.)

By the time December came around, Adam had received his first payment from YouTube. It was the most money he had ever owned in his life! He was still a *long* way from having enough to buy a new car, but it was considerably more than what he'd saved up in the New Gearbox Fund. And if that wasn't already cool enough, Adam had reached an entirely new level of awesomeness – mounted on his bedroom wall was a plaque that had arrived in the post – 'The Play Button' *Presented to Slimeboy AdamYT, for passing 100,000 subscribers.*

Despite all the hundreds of thousands of views and subs, despite the fan mail and the kids waiting to meet him outside school every morning, Adam hadn't ever actually felt like a *real* YouTuber before. That all changed when he received his Play Button. The plaque made it official, and Adam couldn't help but lie in his bed staring at it every night before he fell asleep. And since he had already achieved the impossible 100k milestone, it made it seem all the more plausible that he might also reach the one million milestone too, and receive a *gold* Play Button, to sit beside his silver one.

'*Reach one million by this time next year, or lose all you hold dear*,' Adam recited the message from Popularis, and smiled confidently to himself while tucked under his covers on an exceptionally cold December night. 'I'm going to do this,' he whispered. 'I'm actually going to *do* this!' He felt a warm sensation of pride swell inside him. He wondered if his dad would have been proud of him too.

But mingled with the pride was a strange pang of worry for the weird and magical pop-up ad that had helped him get this far. He hadn't been able to contact Popularis in ages. He'd spent whole evenings scouring the internet for him ... it ... whatever, but it didn't seem to exist anymore. And now that it had vanished, Adam found that he was filled with even more questions than when it had first appeared. *Where has Popularis gone? Didn't it say that it wouldn't be leaving me? Why did it even come to ME in the first place? Will it ever come back?* And the biggest question of all ... *Can I really do this on my own?*

With Popularis missing in action, Adam felt the tiniest bit ... nervous. He wasn't really sure if the computer program *was* magic, but he couldn't deny that it had kick-started his success.

'P-Popularis?' Adam said into the dark room, knowing full well how ridiculous he sounded and hoping that Callum couldn't hear. 'Wherever you are, I just wanted to say thank you.'

He was on his own now.

Except for Derek. Derek was the postman. And Derek the postman was the bearer of *GREAT* news.

10

The Big Con

Derek the postman handed Adam the letter.

Like a dog with a stuffed toy, Adam immediately tore it open.

Then he stood there, hands trembling with excitement, reading it over and over and over again.

WebCon was the biggest gathering of anyone and everyone involved in online video creation – YouTubers and TikTokers, developers, promoters, fans … *lots* of fans. Adam had wanted to go for years, but he'd never been able to afford the flight from Derry to London, or a hotel room, or the ticket. But that was all about to change. WebCon London had *invited* him to go! And not as a fan. They wanted him to be a FEATURED CREATOR!

'No WAY!' Callum gasped when Adam told him the news.

'I know!' Adam gasped right back at him.

'A *Featured Creator*!'

'I know!'

'What *is* a Featured Creator?'

'I don't know!'

'That's awesome!'

'I know!'

It didn't really matter what a Featured Creator was, the important thing was that Adam was *going*. And it was *free*. This letter from Derek the postman was his golden ticket, and in just ten days' time, on December 17th, Adam was going to the YouTube equivalent of the Chocolate Factory! Adam finally felt like he'd hit the big time.

Well, that is until he realised that WebCon had been trying to contact him by email for *weeks*, but they'd had no reply from him. (Having a computer that could barely process emails made Adam feel slightly less than 'Big time'. More like 'Medium time'. Or quite a large 'Small time'.) This was when he decided that if he really was going to be a big-time YouTuber (or 'Creator', as he now knew other big-time YouTubers called themselves) and get hundreds of thousands of subscribers (or '100ks of subs' as other big-time YouTu— *Creators* say) every seven days (or every 'week' as other big-time ... er ... speakers of the English language say), then it was about time he got himself some big-time tech.

'Yes!' Ethan cheered when Adam told him the news in registration. 'You cannot go to WebCon with caveman tech! I've got you, bro! Tech God at your service. Gimme your phone. I know exactly what you need!'

Ethan went into full-on military mode, adding items to Adam's online basket at a fierce rate, listing everything he would need to look the part, act the part – *be* the part.

'This is pricey stuff, Ethan!' Adam's eyes bulged at the total.

'Well, yeah, but it's good quality,' Ethan reasoned. 'No rubbish. Besides, you gotta spend big if you want to *be* big.'

A snort of disdain emanated from behind them.

'You don't want to go with the Canon DSLR, the Lumix is way better. It shoots in 4K.'

The pair spun around to see Bruce Kilter peering over their shoulders. 'I mean, that's what I'd go for if I wanted to be taken seriously,' he added with a nonchalant shrug, before ambling back over to his army of cronies as though giving Adam useful advice was an incredibly normal thing for him to do.

'Er, right. Thanks!' Adam called after him, wondering if he'd woken up in an alternate reality where Bruce 'You Get the Juice' Kilter was no longer the world's worst human being.

'The Lumix *does* look kind of epic,' Adam said uncertainly, his finger hovering over the 'Add' button. 'Is there a new Tech God in school?' he joked as he gave Ethan a nudge with his elbow. He could feel a strange little giggle bubbling up inside him. At the sound of Bruce's voice, Adam's body had braced itself for Fight or Flight, and now it didn't know what to do with all its unused energy except laugh.

But the stony expression on Ethan's face suggested that this was no joke. He had never had his Tech

God credentials called into question before, especially not by Bruce Kilter.

Adam waited until Ethan was fully absorbed in rushing to finish Mr Snidren's History homework before he snuck the Lumix into his basket.

By the next day, Adam had taken delivery of a brand-new computer, a bunch of cameras (two GoPros and the Lumix), some GorillaPods and the best editing software on the market.

A massive, hairy, growling shadow of guilt began following him around when he realised that his 'New Car for Mum Fund' was back down to £0. He knew it made sense though. *How can I grow if I don't improve?* he reasoned to himself. Yes, he felt knotted inside to make his mum have to carry on with that awful journey to work and back every day, but bigger equipment meant bigger videos, and bigger videos meant bigger money, and bigger money meant getting a car even sooner. Yes, it made sense. To him, at least. And Ethan. And, weirdly, Bruce.

In the whirlwind of pre-Christmas chaos,

December 17th arrived in a heartbeat, and with his head still spinning from it all, Adam found himself at Derry airport, boarding a plane to London, along with Mum and Callum, for an adventure of a lifetime.

11

Adam Arrives

Adam's mum was the only member of the family who had been on a plane before. She was also the only member of the family who was a peculiar shade of green as the three of them stepped on to the tarmac of Stansted Airport near London.

'Ha, lovely,' she bluffed as she inhaled a deep gulp of air, as if trying to stop her breakfast from coming back up. 'Right ... ah ... I suppose we ought to make our way to ... Oh dear lord, Adam, what have you done now?'

'Don't tell him!' Adam pleaded through a stifled squeal of laughter. 'It's for a video.'

'Oh well, if it's for a video, please, humiliate your poor little brother all you want,' she joked.

Callum had been far too deeply asleep to notice Adam pranking him on the plane. On the tarmac he was far too busy gawping at all the planes taking off and landing to spot Adam following his every step with his camera. He was having too much fun laughing, dancing and jumping with wide-eyed excitement to notice the group of kids on the escalator chuckle at him or spot the security guard let out a huge belly laugh as he approached. He didn't even notice the old couple at baggage reclaim shake their heads at him in disapproval. But Callum *did* notice the lady in the blue suit almost laugh her sparkling water out of her nose as they passed the café at the arrivals exit.

'First time coming to London?' she asked him as she dabbed the water from her chin.

'Yes! It's awesome!' Callum informed her. 'We *flew* here,' he added, which was possibly not *vital* information, since they were in an *airport* and she was the pilot of their plane.

'Pretty excited, huh?' the pilot said with certainty.

'*Yes!* It's *awesome!*'

Perhaps the pilot knew Callum was excited because he wouldn't stop bouncing up and down all over the place. It could have been because he kept clapping his hands and blurting 'This is *awesome*!' to random strangers. But it was most likely because scrawled across his forehead, in black marker pen, were the words 'I DUN PEE-PEE IN MY PANTS.'

Adam's 'I Pranked My Little Brother While He Slept on the Plane' video was going perfectly.

One person who didn't even crack a smile at the sight of Callum was the suited gentleman outside, waiting patiently by a giant blacked-out Mercedes van and holding a sign that read '*Adam Slimeboy (WebCon)*'.

Mum made a silent 'Oooooooh!' face as they climbed into the rocket-like vehicle. Adam gave a 'Whoa!' at the interior, which looked as though it had been designed with alien technology. And Callum let out an almighty 'AWESOME!' at the built-in games console. Then off they rolled (actually, it felt more like they were *gliding*), and all Adam could think was – *This is just too cool!*

But he didn't mean it in a good way. Suddenly he

really did feel like it was all too cool for him – the flight, the chauffeur, the complimentary hotel … This kind of stuff was for big, famous celebrities, not for a nobody teen who only set up his first YouTube channel two months ago. Not for someone who only got where he was because Popularis had helped him – *cheated* for him. Adam felt like a fraud, an imposter, or as Bruce used to tell him over and over again – a 'loser'. As though someone had invited him by mistake, or out of charity, but definitely not because he *deserved* to be there. He had a growing worry that the WebCon fans might think so too. He could almost hear their voices – '*Who's that?*' – '*What's* he *doing* here?' – '*He's* nobody!' And those worries turned to nightmares as Adam drifted off into the deepest of sleeps.

'OH MY LIFE! IT'S HIM! IT'S ACTUALLY *HIM*!'

Adam jolted awake as Callum screamed in his ear, then frantically clambered over his lap and leaped from the car.

'Wha … ?' Adam groaned in fuzzy-headed confusion.

He glanced out of his window to see what looked like another part of the airport – a huge glass building, all curves and angles.

'Come on, Sleeping Beauty, we're here!' chuckled his mum as she climbed out too.

'Wha … ?' Adam muttered dozily to the empty van.

Where? he wondered. *Did we break down at the airport? Did we have to turn back for something? How long were we driving?*

He checked his watch and was amazed to see that he had slept for almost an *hour*.

'Wha … ?!?!'

His door suddenly flew open and Adam tumbled face-first on to the pavement.

'Whaaaaaaa!'

The driver gestured towards the huge glass building as Adam staggered to his feet.

'The London Azul Hotel, sir.'

Adam looked up to see a forecourt aglow with Christmas lights, lined with fairy-lit trees and buzzing with groups of visitors, all strolling with their wheelie suitcases.

'Whoa!' he whispered.

He stood there, head spinning wildly, trying to take it all in – YouTubers, TikTokers, Instagrammers – everywhere he looked he saw famous faces! And there, right in front of him, Callum's all-time hero – Jack-OJ. And, right in front of Jack-OJ, to Adam's horror, was an electric ball of excitement, bouncing up and down and gasping, 'You're Jack-OJ! Oh my life! You're actually Jack-OJ! This is *awesome*!'

Adam suddenly felt a tiny bit guilty for the whole

'I DUN PEE-PEE IN MY PANTS' prank. He couldn't think of anything more humiliating than meeting your hero while your forehead was secretly decorated with 24-carat embarrassment. But then, as Callum and Jack-OJ posed for a selfie, Adam breathed a sigh of relief to see that Callum's head was now 'PEE-PEE'-free — he must have spotted it in the car and cleaned it off.

'Hey, Slimeboy!' said Jack-OJ, noticing Adam watching them. 'Adam, right? Nice vids, man. I mean it. Seriously cool!'

Adam froze on the spot.

An actual Creator had recognised him!

A real-life YouTuber knew his name!

And had seen his videos!

And ... and ... and was standing there, waiting for Adam to reply, or close his mouth, or maybe even blink.

Adam pulled himself together, racked his brains for what to say, then uttered the coolest and most intelligent thing that came to mind ...

'Err ... hi.'

(Or maybe not.)

Jack-OJ turned as though he were about to head off to the hotel. Then he paused, turned back to Adam, and said, 'Nah, I can't pass this up, come on, we gotta get a selfie together.'

And then, sure as day, Jack-OJ …

Took a selfie!

With Adam!

Jack-OJ gave a brief salute, then off he vanished with his entourage in tow.

Callum gawped at Adam. Then he gawped at Mum. Stunned beyond belief, quivering with adrenalin, Callum whispered –

'Holy … holy … holy …'

Then with a deafening squeal –

'HOLY FLARTS, ADAM, JACK-OJ KNOWS WHO YOU ARE!'

The entire forecourt fell silent as Callum's outburst echoed off the hotel and then off the Expo Arena and then off the towering mountain of embarrassment that was piling out of Adam's very core. But he needn't have worried, because Mum made it all better when, realising her own son had caused a very big scene, she instantly turned a deep shade of scarlet and exercised her skills as a parent—

'Callum!' she spluttered. 'Never, *ever* swear in public!'

'WHAT, FLARTS?!' In his excitement, Callum was continuing to talk at a volume roughly equivalent to that of a ship's foghorn. 'FLARTS ISN'T EVEN A REAL WORD! I MADE IT UP! FLARTS FLARTS FLARTY-FLOOGE FLARTS!'

Adam was out of there like a shot – across the forecourt and inside the hotel before you could even say, '*I've never seen those people before in my life.*'

Once inside the lobby, Adam made the mistake of pausing to pick his jaw up off the floor as he gawped at the opulent interior – marble walls, thick black-and-yellow carpets and a Christmas tree so luxuriant it looked like it belonged in Buckingham Palace – and this momentary pause gave Callum and Mum just enough time to catch up with him.

'F-A-N-C-Y!' Mum mouthed.

'This is *so way* posher than that little caravan we stayed in that time in County Cork!' Callum added.

'Good afternoon, erm, Adam,' said the moustachioed concierge who stepped up to greet them.

Adam was speechless. How did this man know his name? Was he a subscriber? Was he magic? Was Adam's name tag poking out of his pants? Or was this ... *fame?!*

Yes! Adam cheered internally. *I am FAMOUS!*

And, since he was now officially famous, he decided to greet the concierge in the most celebrity-like way he could think of—

'Err ... hi.'

(Or maybe not.)

'This way for WebCon check-in,' said the concierge, ushering Adam towards a private check-in desk.

'This is *so* brilliant!' he whispered to Callum and Mum.

Well, it *was* brilliant until Callum got to the check-in desk and said, 'Greetings to you, my good man!' in his best (and very bad) English accent.

The girl at the desk forced a smile.

Adam tried to make up for Callum's strangeness by dazzling the Desk Girl with some extremely intelligent and hilarious small talk.

'Err ... hi,' he muttered.

(Or maybe not.)

The Desk Girl gave a hysterical snort of laughter before spluttering, 'Oh my days, you're too funny!' Then she pulled out her phone and said, 'OK, shall we do this?' Then, just like Jack-OJ, *she* took a selfie with Adam too.

'Brilliant,' she giggled as she sat back down and began tapping away on her laptop. 'OK, soooo … Adam Beales, plus two …'

Adam tried his hardest to stop grinning from ear to ear, but it was no use, this reception was just too much – everyone seemed to know who he was! Everyone seemed to *love* him!

'Here's your passes,' said the Desk Girl.

Callum squealed with excitement.

'They will get you into the Expo halls,' she continued.

Callum squealed again.

'Keep them with you at all times, they are VIP access all areas.'

Callum's head almost exploded with squeal overload.

The Desk Girl then wrapped the 'Creator' band around Adam's left wrist, and, as casually as if she were commenting on the weather, she dropped a tiny nugget of information that was so monumental it made Adam feel like an army of fairies had crash-landed in his brain, then dropped down to his stomach, where they flew a series of loop-the-loops, before rocketing directly out of his bottom …

'So, Adam, you're nominated for Fastest Growing Creator at the Saturday night YouTube event on the main stage, marked here on your map.'

Stop right there!

Nominated?!

Award?!?!

Main stage??

Adam's brain momentarily derailed, overturned and lay there, on its back, floundering in a pool of its own brain-train fluids.

As the Desk Girl pointed to the map, she couldn't help noticing a piece of chewing gum fall from Adam's wide-open mouth and land directly on her fingertip. There was an awkward moment where she stared at her finger, and Adam stared into oblivion, like a malfunctioned robot. Then there was an even more awkward moment where she raised her gummy finger and said, 'Erm, I think this is yours,' and Adam stared into oblivion like a malfunctioned robot. And the mother of all awkward moments where Adam's mum politely took the chewing gum off the girl's finger, popped it back in Adam's mouth, pushed his jaw closed, mouthed the word 'SORRY' and then the girl said, 'I'm guessing he didn't get the email about that then?' And Adam stared into oblivion like a malfunctioned robot.

'Nominated?' Adam muttered, glassy-eyed, as he shuffled in a zombie-like fashion to their hotel room, pausing every few seconds for yet more selfies.

'*Nominated?*' he repeated as Mum opened their door with the 'F-A-N-C-Y' electronic key card, then helped usher zombified Adam into a room that … a room that … a room that was so utterly unbelievably luxurious that it seemed to sing with the voices of a hundred angels, sparkle with the brilliance of a thousand stars and cause Mum and Callum to recoil in wide-eyed disbelief with the power of a million of those little portable travel fans that you can wear around your neck.

Their room was *beyond* fancy. Their room was barely a room at all, it was more like a *royal suite* – marble bathroom, a TV as big as a bed, reclining armchairs with mini fridges built into the armrests, two bedrooms, a living area *and* a kitchen with one of those fridges that has a built-in ice machine. Aaaaaand … Adam didn't notice *any* of it.

'*Nom … nom … NOMINATED!*' he gasped as Mum and Callum helped lower him on to a sofa.

'Mum … Callum … I did it!' Adam exclaimed, as meek as a mouse, with tears in his eyes. 'People *like* me! People *know my name!* They want *selfies* with me! I'm *not* a fraud! I *do* belong here! I *made* it! I'm actually in the big time! I've *arrived!*'

Mum and Callum shared a look of extreme guilt.

'What?' Adam asked nervously. 'Why are you two looking at each other like that?'

'No reason!' Callum quickly replied.

'Callummmm …' said Mum, warningly. 'Tell him.'

'Tell me what?'

'There's nothing to tell!' insisted Callum. 'Seriously, Adam. All of those people know your name and wanted selfies because you're famous and they love you. End of story.'

'Callum! Tell. Him!'

'What is going on?!' Adam demanded.

'Welllll …' began Callum, squirming uncomfortably on the spot. '*Some* of what happened out there *may* have had something to do with this …'

He held his phone up for Adam to see Instagram, and Adam saw himself staring back. *Lots* of himself. It was Jack-OJ's selfie of the two of them, shared and reposted again and again under the hashtag #SlimeboyAdam. But now he was seeing it one hundred and nineteen times over, he realised there was something strange about it — one tiny little niggling fault, one incey-wincey minuscule issue that made Adam ever so slightly want to disappear into a wormhole and never be seen again. Each and every image included a very clear shot of his forehead, which was beautifully inscribed, in black marker pen, with the words —

#SLIMEBOYADAM SELFIE TIME! (I DUN BIG POO-POO IN MY PANTS)

'Sorry,' said Callum, wincing in discomfort, 'I kind of pranked you back when you were asleep in the car.'

Every fibre of Adam's being screamed out in horror, yet his mouth only managed three simple words ...

'Kill me now.'

12

Find Callum

Adam was funny. Adam did silly things. Thankfully, because Adam was funny and because Adam did silly things, the internet had decided that he had written on his own forehead as a funny, silly joke. And this joke had caused his online following to shoot up overnight. So, luckily for Callum, Adam forgave him. But Adam wasn't going to tell him this because:

A – Callum was still asleep
B – It's never a good idea to congratulate your little brother for writing 'poo-poo' on your forehead (he might make a habit of it).

Adam sat there, in the fanciest hotel suite, on the poshest sofa, browsing endless channels on the biggest TV, but he found he couldn't enjoy any of it because—

'I ought to be making a video of this!' he barked at himself. 'Why didn't I plan anything? We're at *WebCon*! We're in this massive hotel – the perfect place for some big videos – and I've done nothing!'

But no matter how hard Adam racked his brains, no good video ideas were coming to mind, until –

The TV screen suddenly went black. Then it flashed white. Blindingly bright, just as his computer screen had done on the night he'd summoned Popularis.

FLASH!

A jolt of electricity kicked him in the brain.

FLASH!

A deafening screech tore at his ears.

FLAAAAAAASH!

Adam had curled into a ball on the floor, with his arms over his head. When he finally looked up, he saw cartoons back on the TV, and all was normal. Well, *almost* normal – there on the bottom of the screen, where it usually had a scrolling message to tell you what programme was up next, was a different message altogether …

Don't lose Callum … Don't lose Callum … Don't lose Callum …

Popularis Incrementum had returned.

Adam's heart began to race, for a million reasons – shock, adrenalin, panic …

Don't lose Callum?! Is he missing? Is he in danger?

Adam jumped out of his seat, and then, as if on cue, Callum came shuffling out of the bedroom, rubbing his eyes and scratching his head. And that's when Adam realised that the message wasn't a warning, it was *a clue* – a clue to what his next video should be!

A smile spread across Adam's face, and he knew instantly that he had another banger on his hands.

13

Hide-and-Seek

It's so simple it's almost stupid, Adam thought to himself. *And it's so stupid it's almost genius*. And those thoughts were such a load of gibberish they almost made sense. 'Don't lose Callum,' Adam realised, was Popularis Incrementum's way of telling him to film a 'Hide-and-Seek' video (stupid) in a massive hotel (genius).

Thirty minutes later they were standing outside the hotel armed with cameras.

'Hey guys, it's me, Slimeboy Adam, and today we're gonna be playing ...' The camera rotated in Adam's hand to reveal the impressive structure behind them. 'Hide-and-seek in a luxury London hotellllll!'

123

The imposing structure looked stunning in the camera viewfinder – definitely worth a click to a discerning viewer. He could already envision the video thumbnail.

'And today I'm joined by … Callum!'

His little body and large head looked even funnier in the viewfinder.

'Now, Callum, old chum old pal –' (OK, so Adam's English accent was maybe even worse than his little brother's) '– do you understand the rules? It's pretty simple. We'll take it in turns to go hide, while the other has to, well, errr, yep, you guessed it. Seek! We seek him here, we seek him there, we seek-a seek-a seek-a seek him EV-ERY-WHERE!' He was really finding his flow now. So much so that he'd slipped into a patented Adam Beales Whirlwind of Annoyingness Annoyingly Catchy Song TM. It turned out that his fans loved them (although so far he'd refrained from treating them to the accompanying dance).

'And guys,' Adam went on, reining in the warbling, 'if you like this video, don't forget to like and subscribe! So, yeah, without further ado, let's start the videoooooooooo!'

So, without further ado, Adam started the video ... Well, technically there was a *bit* of ado, truth be told, while Adam made sure he had all the shots of the hotel he needed to splice together when he edited his footage later ...

So, with little-to-no further ado ... err, no, scratch that, because by then Callum needed a wee and had to ride the lift up nineteen floors to their room before coming all the way back down again, and then he thought he saw Jack-OJ going into the swanky ground-floor restaurant, so he hovered around the entrance for twenty minutes hoping he could 'accidentally' bump into him again on the way out ...

So, with quite a lot of further ado overall, actually, Adam started the video.

Adam darted off first, GoPro in hand, recording his live-action footage, while Callum stayed behind with the larger Lumix. (Adam had to admit that it had been great advice from Bruce. The 4K quality was superb.)

'Guys, it's a tight fit but ... yep ... I'm in!' Adam struggled to maintain camera-to-face action as he climbed into a very, very small cupboard at the end of the very, very large reception desk in the foyer.

His efforts had drawn the gaze of several other Creators. A gaggle of them were watching on from the impossibly pillowy chairs in the front lounge, laughing at the young contortionist twisting his lanky frame in all directions to make it fit, like he was playing human Tetris.

(*Mental note*, Adam thought, desperately using the only finger that wasn't engaged in keeping the cupboard closed to free a chunk of his unruly hair from where it had got caught in the hinge of the door when he'd pressed his face against it. *Human Tetris would make an EPIC future Slimeboy video!*)

Callum would never have found Adam by himself, but luckily he was able to rely on eager wannabe participants giving him *strong* hints each time he flew past Adam's secret location.

'GOTCHA! OK, my turn!'

Adam unfolded himself just in time to see Callum racing off, breathless with the effort, to find his own hiding place, followed by twenty Creators and somebody's dog.

The result was golden content, Adam just knew it. Fifteen madcap minutes of hide-and-seek heaven in a sequence of increasingly bizarre hiding locations – changing room lockers, linen closets, between two oversized plant pots, behind an oversized plant pot, *inside* an oversized plant pot, the sauna, the steam room, the swimming pool showers, on top of the housekeeping trolley, and, finally, inside the hotel room of an extremely angry man with an extremely bald head and an extremely orange bathrobe ...

'OK! Work is done! To the Expo hall!' cheered Callum as they made it back to their room. 'All the BIG creators will be there! Let's dump the tech and go *now* or the crowds will be MASSIVE!'

'Callum, just cool it, OK? Gimme thirty mins to edit this. I need it done today.' Adam's voice couldn't hide a hint of irritation.

Callum slumped on the bed with a deep sigh of 'I-wanna-go-to-WebCon-ness'.

By lunchtime, Adam had the whole video finished and ready to go up on YouTube later that day. Sensing the editing activity decrease – no more *tappity-tap* of the keyboard, no more *grr-bbit-bit-grrr* of video segments being dragged around the software at high speed – Callum popped up again like a meerkat.

'Yes! Fiiinallly! Let's go!'

'Not ... riiight ... now. I just need to finish off a few more things,' Adam muttered.

Callum smashed both palms into his forehead.

'How much longer?! The greatest party in the world is just outside, and we're stuck in here, in the most boring blah of nothing in the world!'

But Adam was too busy to reply.

Forty minutes after that, Adam had his 'I dun pee-pee' prank on Callum ready to go up for the next day. And then he saw the folder full of 'poo-poo' prank footage Callum had sneakily filmed of *him* ...

'You, my friend, are going straight to the trash,' Adam told the video (he talked to videos way more than was healthy). But just as he was about to press delete, the screen of the camera suddenly glowed a blinding white.

'Now?' he managed to utter before –

FLASH!

A jolt of electricity kicked him in the brain.

FLASH!

A deafening screech tore at his ears.

FLAAAASSHHHH!

The piercing digital shriek rang through Adam's head once again, and he found himself on his knees, the camera still in his hands and the screen now blinking a warning message –

! BATTERY LOW !
GO WITH YOUR BROTHER

Adam groaned. Any fleeting excitement Adam had felt at Popularis returning to help him twice in one day quickly drained away as he figured out what that message meant – it was telling him to go with Callum's video. To edit it and actually put it on YouTube.

Adam gave another groan when he realised that Popularis was totally right – Callum's video would absolutely be a banger. Yes, it would be humiliating and horribly embarrassing, but he had to admit – it would be a funny video. *Very* funny! So he swallowed his pride, edited the footage and scheduled it to be published two days later. Three videos in one day! No-upload Guilt removed! Not bad, considering he was only there for an awards ceremony ... Wait ... the awards ...

They start in thirty minutes!

Adam had been so distracted making videos that he'd completely missed *hours* of WebCon fun – Q&As, meet-and-greets, signings – and now he had to shower, get changed and find his way to the Expo hall in double-quick time! And not just him ...

'MUM! CALLUM! WE'RE LATE!' In a blind panic, Adam raced out of his room to find Mum making a cup of tea, looking stunned. And Callum was ... Callum was ... 'Wait ... Mum, where's Callum?'

'Ha ha, very funny, Adam – but you're not getting me with the 'I've Lost Callum' prank. Not again. It *is* an 'I've Lost Callum prank', right? Tell me it's an 'I've Lost Callum' prank!'

Adam had done a lot of searching that day, but none had been as frantic as this.

They searched the bedrooms.

No Callum.

They searched the entire suite.

No Callum.

They searched the hallways outside their room, the vending machines, the lifts …

No Callum!

The only thing they found was his phone, on the floor, next to the sofa.

'Please don't tell me he went into WebCon without us,' Adam muttered in panic.

'Adam, no,' his mum whispered, turning grey. 'It's so crowded in there! And he's so little! And he doesn't even have his phone!'

'Come on, we have to go to the awards,' said Adam, heading back to the lifts. 'Let's find him on the way!'

'We can't! Not *both* of us! What if he comes back to the room? He doesn't have a key!'

Adam growled with frustration. 'OK,' he agreed. 'I'll go. You wait here for him. Come to the awards *as soon* as he gets back.'

But Adam had a feeling neither of them would be making it to his awards. He had a bad feeling about the whole thing.

14

Expo(sed)

'Adam! Adam! Look, it's Slimeboy Adam!'

Adam was in too much of a panic to stop for fans. Just like the vast, crowded Expo hall, his head was full of noise, with all the emotions pushing to get to the front. Anger was elbowing its way through the bustle, stuffing its face on a Selfish-Callum-for-Disappearing burger. Guilt was wandering around, with tears in its eyes, thinking that Callum had only disappeared in the first place because Adam hadn't taken good enough care of him. And big old lumbering sadness was trudging all over the other emotions, squashing them against the walls, stepping on toes and wishing it could see Mum's face light up at the 'F-A-N-C-Y' awards ceremony instead of being stuck back in their room.

The place was so big and hard to navigate. The amusement rides were spinny, the queues long and snaky, the screens blindingly bright ... and suddenly there it was, the largest screen of all, like a departures board in an airport, listing all the upcoming events, where they could be found and how many hours and minutes until they started. Right at the very top of the screen was *Adam's* event – YouTube Awards, Main Stage, *1 MINUTE*!

BAM! Panic burst into the room, shoved all other emotions out of its way and began racing around, smashing into things, like a bull in a very, very, very crowded Expo hall! He had to find the backstage entrance to the Main Stage, FAST! What if his award was up first? What if he *won* and he wasn't there?!

He rushed this way and that, his heart racing, his temperature soaring. Everything was so loud! So busy! So *whirly*! And then he tripped ...

The gigantic foot of the towering security guard spread across the hall like a sprawling root from a tree. Adam stumbled over the root-foot, crashed straight through a doorway and found himself in a darkened hall. Dozens of faces all turned to see who had disturbed their show. And that's when he realised where he was. He had literally stumbled across the exact place he'd been searching for – the VIP Area off the Main Stage.

Gradually the sea of YouTubers, Instagrammers and TikTokers sitting at food-laden tables turned their attention back to the stage, where the presenter was finishing off his introduction.

Adam wandered around like a lost schoolboy as

he searched for an empty seat. He noticed that all the other Creators seemed to know each other, and that he didn't seem to fit in. Then he noticed that there wasn't a single empty seat at any of the tables and that he *literally* wasn't going to fit in.

Head down, he thought, like the VIP area was the school corridor and every Creator was Bruce. *Don't react*. But then –

'Hey! Poopy Pants! Adam! Come and sit with us!'

Two other Creators were eagerly beckoning Adam over to their table.

They were a couple of years older than Adam and both as overexcited as fourteen Callums rolled into one. Joanne and Lee were their names, and, far from making him feel like an outsider, they instantly proved to be the most brain-meltingly hilarious people Adam had ever met in his life.

Within twenty minutes, they'd made him laugh more than he'd laughed all *year*:

- in homage to him, they both happily picked up marker pens and wrote '#Poopy pants' on their foreheads

- Joanne sent a 'Missing you! Love you LOADS! XXX' message to her mum, but accidentally sent it to her driving instructor
- Lee hiccuped so violently that he fell off his chair (which made Adam and Joanne *laugh* so violently that they fell off *their* chairs)!

Joanne and Lee were the perfect antidote for Adam's nervousness, and before long he had almost forgotten how much he was missing Mum and Callum.

And then it happened.

Joanne and Lee started bouncing up and down in their seats and wildly tapping Adam on his shoulders in a frenzy of anticipation.

'It's *time*!' explained Lee, in response to Adam's expression of saucer-eyed confusion.

'Your category!' added Joanne, just as the compere said the words 'award for fastest growing Creator!'

Adam's stomach lurched. His head spun. His category was about to be announced! He hoped he would win – he didn't want to lose in front of so many people. He hoped he would *lose* – he didn't want to get up in front of so many people! He hoped …

Adam's heart jolted as he spotted a little familiar-looking bean head bobbing through the crowd a few metres away, just beyond the VIP area.

'Heyyyy!' The top of Callum's curly hair was only just visible among the sea of spectators.

Joanne and Lee cocked their necks like a pair of hens as Adam bounced out of his seat and ran over, pushing over chairs, scattering drinks and banging into tables. Perhaps his 'as-the-crow-flies' approach wasn't the subtlest, but it got him to his little brother's side in a flash.

'Callum, what the Jeff! Where were you? Mum's worried sick! And I—'

But before Adam could chastise him any further, Callum screamed and grabbed Adam's arm.

'THIS IS IT, ADAM!' He seemed totally oblivious to the chaos he had caused. 'Fastest-growing creator! This is you!'

Incoming call.

Adam's phone was glitching like mad. Half the screen was black, showing no caller ID, the other

half had been shunted downwards. Adam was beginning to realise why Bruce had been so quick to be
rid of it! It was turning out to be an old banger of a
phone! (The bad kind of banger.) But Adam didn't
need caller ID, he already knew who it was.

'MUM! I found Callum! He's here with me! It's
my category *right now*! If you hurry, you might make
it! We're in —'

'Adam, mate, it's *me*,' replied a voice that was
definitely not his mum.

Adam couldn't believe his ears.

'*Bruce?*'

'I'm watching on the WebCon live stream! Your
category is up! Listen, man, good luck! I really hope
you w—'

And then the call cut out completely, the screen
continuing to glitch between the home screen and
complete blackness.

Adam was dizzy with confusion. Had *Bruce Kilter*,
his sworn enemy and ultimate nemesis, really just
called him? Called to say … called to say what?
'I really hope you w-w-w-whiff up your next video
and lose all your followers? W-w-w-walk straight

under the tracks of a passing tank? W-w-wake up with toes where your fingers should be and fingers where your toes should be?' These all seemed far likelier than what it *sounded* like he was going to say – 'I really hope you *win*.' Surely Bruce Kilter would *never* say that?

But Adam had no time to ponder it further.

'The Award for Fastest-Growing Creator goes to …'

15

The Loser

Joanne and Lee ran over and pounced on to Adam's back. They ruffled his hair with pride. They slapped his shoulders in congratulation. They nuzzled his ears with weird ... erm ... strangeness. Then they leaped off him and launched him towards the stage, where he almost fell flat on his face.

Adam could not believe it. But it was true. It had actually happened. He could still hear his name ringing out through the hall.

'Adam!' he could hear Callum squealing. 'You *won*! YOU WON!'

Adam's jelly legs began walking up the steps. A stage assistant accompanied him and asked if he minded if they synched his phone camera to the big screen display on the stage. 'You'll get to be the live camera operator for a few minutes,' she explained, 'letting everyone see your point of view.'

In a daze, Adam agreed, and in four seconds flat the assistant had wirelessly hooked his phone to the big screen, and the audience was treated to a thirty-foot close-up of Adam's nostrils and flaming-red cheeks. (But at least the footage remained glitch-free.) He realised he should probably flip the view, but the crowd seemed to be loving it, laughing their heads off, like he was being a goof on purpose. So he rolled with it and gifted them a feast of unflattering close-ups.

To his huge surprise, Adam found that his legs were no longer jelly. His heart was no longer racing. He was ... *enjoying it*!

'A YouTube sensation, and photogenic too!' joked the presenter as he handed Adam his award, along with a painful slap of congratulations on his back.

'Thank you!' Adam cheered into the mic on the lectern, giving the crowd a wide-angle shot of themselves as he held his award and his phone aloft, like a monkey on a mountain with a newborn lion. 'Thank you so much! I'd just like to say ...'

Adam froze in terror.

Someone had interrupted him.

A voice from behind blared out at an ear-shredding volume.

The voice of the worst person Adam could ever imagine interrupting him—

Himself.

There he was, up on the big screen, two years younger, four times bigger, wearing a massive nappy and dancing wildly in his bedroom as he sang 'HEYYYYY NAPPY-RENA! AYEEE!'

His phone was no longer transmitting a live feed from his camera, it was playing old videos from his cloud storage!

The audience erupted in laughter as real Adam jabbed furiously at his phone, desperately trying to stop the horror that was playing out behind him. But the device seemed to have a mind of its own and no matter what Adam tried, he could not make it stop.

Then it did stop. All by itself.

The big screen cut to blackness.

The hysterical crowd calmed to a hushed murmur of curiosity as they waited for Adam to say something.

But Adam's brain was a car crash of confusion.

The silence seemed to drag on for an eternity.

'Well ...' he said at last, 'I ... Ermm ... Hah. And you guys thought the whole "poo-poo in my pants" thing was embarrassing!'

It worked. The crowd roared with laughter and Adam hurried backstage with a grateful wave.

It wasn't enough though. Sure, he'd managed to trick the audience into thinking it was all just another joke, but Adam had a horrible feeling that his embarrassment had been caused by more than just a glitching phone – the timing was too perfect, the 'Nappy-rena' video too mortifying. The whole thing felt as though it had been planned.

A niggly, wiggly little maggot of doubt crept into Adam's brain.

Popularis, was this you?

Adam tried to dismiss it – after all, Popularis was his friend, his YouTube accomplice, not some scheming saboteur, right? The maggot of doubt wiggled faster. Had this pop-up ad, or AI, or whatever it was, simply been lulling him into a false sense of security all these weeks? Building him up, only to have him humiliated and beaten down at any point in time?

Maybe the advice it provides comes at a price?

Adam was in full-blown mental FBI agent mode, tussling with Popularis's possible motives. The whole thi—

Adam's phone gave three short buzzes. It was a video message from Bruce.

'Hey, Adam, we got cut off just now, so I thought I'd send you a vid, just to make sure you got the message.' Bruce had obviously filmed it as he wandered through his immense mansion, which Adam could see, in all its swanky glory, over Bruce's shoulder. His room was huge, his TV was huge, his house was huge, his dad's huge collection of vintage cars, outside on their huge drive, was huge … *'Anyway, just wanted to wish you luck. I found your category on the WebCon Twitter feed, and saw you were up for an award, and you really deserve to win, man. Your vids are killer, man. I mean it. Anyway, that's all. Laters, bro.'*

Adam was confused. That video was … well … it was *quite nice* really. Not the kind of thing Bruce would send at all! Why was everyone behaving like they'd had personality transplants?

Bruce sending nice messages …

Ethan sending *no* messages …

Callum almost ruining his big moment …

And Popularis? Well … Adam didn't know what to think. All he knew was that he wouldn't be asking for its help again any time soon.

16

Unremarkably Normal

Going back to school after the Christmas holidays was rubbish. All the fun was over. No more gifts, games, films, food, family, late nights and fairy lights. And, for Adam at least, no more squealing fans, fancy hotels, chauffeur-driven space cars, first-class flights and *prestigious awards*. Hello grey skies, soggy lunchbox sandwiches and Mr Snidren's history class.

As he sat staring out of the classroom window, listening to Snidren's droning voice bore a hole into the back of his brain, Adam didn't *feel* like a YouTube sensation, he felt just like his old, unproductive self. He felt completely and utterly unremarkably normal.

Adam's only solace was that the summer holidays were only five months away. Eight lovely long weeks with nothing to do but plan videos, each more epic than the last. Eight weeks without Snidren's mind-numbing history lessons! Eight weeks free from those fun-zapping, gut-wrenching, panic-inducing words – 'Adam! Bed! You've got school in the morning!' Adam could picture it now ...

'And the award for Most Miserable Kid in Class goes to ... *Slimeboy Adam*! Wooooo! Yeeaaaaahhh!' Usually Adam found Ethan's constant stream of commentary comforting, but today it was getting on his nerves.

Mr Snidren seemed to share that sentiment.

'I'm sorry, Ethan,' Snidren sneered. 'I didn't realise it was your turn to speak. I thought *I* was conducting this lesson. Unless, of course, you want to take over?'

If Mr Snidren thought this would send Ethan sheepishly running for cover, it didn't quite have the desired effect ...

'Me? *Take the class?* Are you *serious*?! That's the

best idea I've ever heard! We could start with the history of pancakes – that would be a practical part of the lesson, then we could move on to the history of television, where we could study some of the finest examples of Japanese animation, and then …'

'Forget I spoke,' Snidren interrupted. 'Just please stop talking.'

The words 'stop talking' did not appear in Ethan's vocabulary. But he did at least bring his non-stop verbal tsunami down to an acceptable whisper.

'C'mon!' he hissed in Adam's ear. 'You won an *award* last month! You should be swinging from lamp posts, not wallowing in despair like your cat just died! Wait … your cat *didn't* just die, did it? Hang on, you don't even have a cat. Or do you? Did you get a cat for Christmas and you didn't even tell me? A dead one? I have no idea, you never tell me *anything* any more. Maybe I should ask Bruce. You *can* tell me things, you know? Like, how *I* could become a YouTube sensation overnight too. Or what it feels like to be the most famous person in the history of our school. Or, like, you know, why you're the most miserable person on Earth, when you should be the happiest! We *can* talk still, like old times. Talking is *good*. Or talk to *someone* at least! Your mum! Even *Callum*. Express yourself! You never know, it might actually make you feel less angry. Or are you just sad? Sadam? *Mad*am? *Bad*am?'

The truth was, Adam wasn't too sure what was making him Sadam/Madam/Badam. Normality? Boredom? The fact that he hadn't dared try to contact Popularis since the whole WebCon Nappy-rena nightmare?

Or was it that Popularis hadn't tried to contact *him*?

It did feel a bit like Popularis was *punishing* him for being suspicious of it. Acting like a jealous bitter friend.

Well, I'm RIGHT to be suspicious of you, Popularis! Adam thought.*You're a mysterious voice on the internet! I don't know anything about you! I can't believe I wasn't more suspicious of you from the start!*

All Adam knew for sure was that it wasn't just

him that was suffering. His videos were too. As the weeks went by and January bumped into February, his subscriber count went down. And so did his mum's new car fund.

One especially dreary February afternoon, Adam sat at his kitchen table, staring at his beans on toast, listening to some awful TV show his mum was watching about hits from the 1980s, and wished, *prayed* that he could just feel his dad's hands on his shoulders and hear his voice whispering in that deep way that he used to, '*Hey, buddy, love you one million.*'

But it didn't happen.

Instead, he got – 'Oh, Adam, *please* stop moping around! I wish you would just tell me what's both-ering you!'

Adam knew Ethan was right. He really ought to talk to his mum, let her know what was going on inside his head, but he didn't feel like it. There was only one person Adam felt he might have been able to confide in about what he was going through, and that clearly wasn't going to happen.

'You've not even touched your dinner!' Mum

disappeared up the stairs, but her voice carried on making itself heard even once she was at the top. 'Please don't waste it, I gave you a whole tin of beans!'

But Adam didn't feel like eating. He pushed his plate away. He tried to get up from his seat, but the room started spinning. His ears were ringing. And all the lights seemed too bright. Especially the TV. It was *really* bright. Like, *blinding*. It almost seemed like …

FLASH!

A jolt of electricity kicked him in the brain.

FLASH!

A deafening screech tore at his ears.

FLAAAASSSHHHHHH!

Adam's legs buckled under him. He had one hand in his beans on toast, and he couldn't stop staring at the TV screen, which was playing the same section of music video over and over again, like a stuck record – '*Express yourself – express yourself – express yourself …*'

'What are you trying to tell me, Popularis?' Adam whispered. 'I don't hear from you for months on end, and then you show up with a *song*? How is this going to help me reach one million?'

But then a memory sparked in Adam's mind ... He knew that song! Yes! It had been playing in the garage the day Dad had showed him the Coke and Mentos trick!

'*Just a normal, boring, unbranded bottle of Coke, right?*' his dad had said. '*And just an average, unremarkable pack of regular Mentos, yeah? Neither of them doing anything fun. Both just sitting around, getting bored. But look what happens if you mix it up a bit* ...' His dad held the opened pack of Mentos over the open Coke bottle. '*You soon come to realise that, in actual fact, there is no such thing as boring or unremarkable or average* ...' He squeezed the entire pack of Mentos into the bottle, then jumped back as one of the many wonders of the world took place before their very eyes – a geyser of frothing Coke shot so high out of the bottle that it hit the garage ceiling!

'Would you get your hand out of your beans!' snapped Adam's mum, yanking him out of his memory. 'What on earth are you playing at?!'

'YES!' Adam whooped in delight. 'THANK YOU, POPULARIS!'

He shovelled handful after handful of cold beans into his mouth before darting upstairs in a frenzy of excitement.

'*I* am an unremarkable, normal bottle of Coke!' he could be heard exclaiming from inside his room. 'I just need to add some Mentos!'

Just like that, Adam had come up with the perfect plan to put his life and his channel back on track.

'This is going to be AMAAAZIIIING!'

His mum blinked in astonishment.

'Feeling better then?' she said to the empty room.

17

Absolutely Mento

Adam was fizzing with excitement. Bubbling with energy! Bursting with eagerness as he bounced up and down on his bed.

'You've been so lazy!' he yelled into his mirror. 'All these people doing things for you – free rides, free phone, free fancy hotel, free first-class flights – and you've been sitting back, doing nothing, like a pack of Mentos and a bottle of Coke just sitting on a shelf! But I'm a Creator! I need to *create*! I need to drop Mentos into my life, and seriously shake things up!'

So, the very next day, that's exactly what he did.

- Instead of waiting for someone to invite him to sit on the second-to-last row at the back of

the class, he invited *himself*. To the *very back
row*. He found himself sitting next to Bruce
Kilter for the rest of the day. And the two of
them actually, sorta, kinda hit it off. It turned
out Bruce was nearly as obsessed with
YouTubers as Adam. Bruce even had his own
channel, and it was nice for Adam to talk to
someone who was as invested in creating
content as he was. Sure, it wasn't easy
pretending not to notice the puppy-dog eyes
that Ethan kept shooting his way from four
rows in front, and it was even harder to ignore
the messages on his phone – 'So … Adam …
when I said you should talk more … this
isn't exactly what I had in mind.' But Adam
wasn't about to let old friends hold him
back. He was on a roll! And speaking of
old friends …

- Instead of waiting for good video ideas to be
handed to him by Popularis, he sat himself
down with a notebook and he brainstormed,
researched, found inspiration, and he didn't
stop until he had a plan for a brand-new video

for every single day of the next month. And he didn't just stop at 'brand-new' videos …

- If there was one thing he *had* learned from Popularis, it was that making a fool of himself wasn't always a bad thing. In fact, Adam's most embarrassing moments were usually his biggest (not including the 'Nappy-rena' thing. That was just horrible. And mean). So instead of *fearing* embarrassment, Adam decided to *embrace* it. He was going to take control of his own destiny! It wouldn't be possible for anyone else to embarrass him if he got there first. He was going to take back the power and upload all of his old videos – the more embarrassing the better!

But uploading embarrassing old videos was only the beginning – that was just 'one Mento at a time' kind of stuff. Adam knew that in order to create a huge reaction he would have to drop the entire *pack* of Mentos into his life. Metaphorically speaking. And he knew exactly how he was going to do it.

18

The Big Fizz

Adam could have tried to explain the amazing-ness of the swimming pool by rhyming it with 'cool', but that would have been way too lame. He could have used 'amazing' to describe how the sun was blazing, but that would have been even lamer. He could have tried to express the ultra-modern trendiness of the villa by saying it was 'killa', but really, Callum summed the whole thing up best when he said –

'OH MY JIFFA-WAGGA-HOOCHIE-BAMBO-GEEEENAAAAA! THIS IS … THIS IS … THIS IS … WWWWOOOOOOWWWWW!'

Adam's 'I Took My Family on a Mystery Holiday' video was definitely the full pack of Mentos his bottle-of-cola life had been screaming for. It had started with Mum and Callum packing their bags, with no idea of where they were going ('Give me some kind of clue, Adam! Should I pack snow boots or snorkels?' Mum had pleaded), followed by a drive to their first surprise location – the airport, followed by another surprise, a *whopper* of a surprise – A PRIVATE JET! All to themselves!

Callum had been completely lost for words. All except one – he must have said 'awesome' more times in ten minutes than most other people do in their entire lives. The steps on to the plane were 'awesome', the lighting inside it was 'awesome', the marble sink in the toilet was 'awesome', the reclining luxury armchairs, the super-long sofas, the mini fridges stocked with every drink imagin-able, the cupboards loaded with snacks and sweets, the polished mahogany interior, the armrest control panels for the lights, the seat adjustments, the blinds, the drop-down cinema screen – all 'awesome with extra awesome sauce'.

As the plane touched down, the pilot had finally let Mum and Callum know where they were.

'Thank you for flying with us today, and we hope you have a pleasant stay in Ibiza.'

'*Ibiza?*' Mum squealed. '*IBIZA?!*'

'AWESOME!' cheered Callum, punching the air. 'IBIZA! Hang on, where's Ibiza?'

And the surprises did not stop there. As they stepped off the plane they were greeted with a stretch limo that was waiting for them *on the tarmac*. And that luxury limousine drove them to the final surprise of the journey – the mother of all villas (which really was killa)! Set into the side of a hill, overlooking the ocean, it was the size of a small hotel, and best of all – it had its own private pool.

Adam felt a glowing sensation inside to see Mum and Callum so happy. This holiday was the deal of a lifetime, and it was his hard work that had made it all possible. First, *MOD-JETS* had reached out, offering return flights in exchange for a link to their services in the text beneath one of Adam's videos. Then swanky accommodation company *Villas Direct* had done the same, and thrown in limo transfers from the airport for good measure.

Adam was starting to see how the big creators financed their lavish lifestyles. This was essentially a *free* holiday, and it felt mind-bogglingly brilliant!

So, to make sure his first 'I Took My Family on a Mystery Holiday' video got the ending it deserved, Adam opened the villa gates, calmly removed his shoes, then, with his action cam in hand, he went racing up to the front of the villa, took a flying leap from a raised flower bed and dived straight into the gigantic swimming pool.

'MY NAME IS ADAM BEALES, AND I AM A HUMAN MENTO!'

Once they had taken the grand tour of the place, which was fancy beyond all reasonable sense (every bedroom was en suite, the stairs lit up one step at a time when you walked on them, the kitchen had six different types of fizzy drink on tap, the basement had *three* games rooms, there was a sauna, a Jacuzzi, an infinity pool with surfboards), the three of them spent the evening gazing at the stars and munching on pizza in the heated pool. At this point, Callum had not shut up about how 'awesome' the villa was for three hours straight.

'It is though, right? It's just ... so ...'

'Awesome?' Adam guessed.

'I mean, we thought Mr and Mrs O'Bannon's freezing-cold, leaf-filled pool was nice!' Callum continued. 'Compared to this, their pool is just an oversized pond!'

'I think it's fair to say that, after the year we've had, we well and truly deserve this,' said Mum,

barely visible through the steam rising off the pool. 'Thank you, Adam.'

'Mum, the things you do for us, you deserve this every single day. I love you, Mum. I love you one mil— one heck of a lot,' said Adam, the mist in his eyes so thick that he almost said the one phrase he'd promised himself he would never utter.

It was the best first day of any holiday in the entire history of first days of holidays. But all three of them were wrecked from their day of travelling, and it wasn't long before they each went to their unbelievably huge bed in their unbelievably huge bedroom.

'So, guys, here I am – Slimeboy Adam, at the mystery location for my latest video, which is going to drop TO-MOR-ROW!' Adam announced to his camera as he flung himself backwards on to his bed. 'It is going to be *big*. And when I say *big*, I mean it is going to be HUUUUUUUUUG! And it's not just tomorrow – I've got a brand-new video every day this week. So watch this space, because – trust me – this week is going to get *MEGA*!'

Adam signed off, uploaded his teaser video, then

immediately published it to his channel and watched the comments come flooding in —

- OMG I CAN'T WAIT!!! 👍 103 👎
- Slimeboy Adam is planning a BIG ONE 👍 94 👎
- I am literally just going to stare at my screen until your next videos go online 👍 82 👎
- Can't wait. The new Ed Almighty has arrived! 👍 178 👎
- I HAVE to know what your next videos are going to be! The anticipation is giving me a heart attack! 👍 111 👎

The pressure was officially on. Adam prayed that his next videos would all go to plan, because he did *not* want to disappoint his fans. Speaking of which ... Hearing Callum gently snoring from the next room made him wondered if his little brother had found the 'gift' that Adam had left on his bed — a prop, ready for one of tomorrow's mega-videos.

Adam crept out of his room, silently pushed

Callum's door open, then pointed his camera in through the opening to get a shot of Callum curled up on his bed, his arms wrapped around a gigantic, six-foot teddy bear.

'Look at little Bean Head,' Adam whispered to the camera. 'I think he likes his present. Don't those two look sooooo cute together? I almost feel bad about the prank I've got planned for them tomorrow night!'

Adam was feeling on top of the world as he padded back down the corridor to his room. He grabbed his phone to scroll through all his footage. His phone was the only piece of tech he was allowed to take on the plane, so he'd used it to capture every single one of the day's events. Except there was one problem. There were no videos. Not a single one! Gone! Disappeared! Deleted! Never to be seen again!

Adam felt like he was going to be sick. His glitchy phone had struck again.

'NOOOOO!' he roared as he threw himself back on to his bed. 'Why? Why? WHY?!'

He lay there, constantly searching his phone, turning it off then on again, checking and rechecking his cloud storage, but his videos never reappeared. A cocktail of anger and confused self-pity exploded inside him, and he hurled his phone across the room.

All that time and effort spent on a private jet. The villa too – wasted. The entire amazing day – ruined. And to make matters worse, Adam had now broken the Golden Rule of Social Media – he'd *future-click-baited* everyone! He had promised a video that he didn't have!

Teasing your fans but never delivering? That was social self-implosion, a big greasy fat no-no. And as an extra kick in the teeth, it meant that he couldn't trust his phone for the rest of the holiday! For the rest of *ever*!

As soon as they got home, he would have to use up even more of Mum's new car fund to get himself a phone that he could rely on.

But rather than let it crush him, Adam fed on this frustration, and it made him more determined than ever that tomorrow's vids were going to make up for today's loss. Tomorrow's vids were going to be HUGE.

They *had* to be.

19

Slow Down

It was going to be a great big, fast-paced, action-packed, fun-fuelled, non-stop, wham-bam-alakazzam, epic roller coaster ride of a day, and it wasn't going to stop until the sun hit the horizon and heads hit the pillows.

Except for the morning. Adam's only plans for the morning were exactly this – nothing. A big fat dollop of nothing, followed by a nice juicy chunk of nothing, with a sprinkling of nothing on the side and a drizzly splurge of nothing lazily plopped on top. Exceeeeeept ... Since he had lost an entire video, he didn't really feel like he actually deserved to do nothing.

Yesterday's frustration and disappointment still clung to Adam like stray hairs in a swimming pool, and no matter how hard he tried, he just could not shake them off. So, in a last-minute change of plan, instead of doing *nothing*, Adam decided to do a bit of *something* instead. Something that began with 'V' and rhymed with 'biddy-oh'. And nothing screamed 'the-perfect-replacement-for-a-private-jet-video-that-cost-thousands-of-pounds' more than ... his bedroom window.

OK, not *exactly* his bedroom window, that would be silly. It was the BALCONY *outside* his bedroom window that had Adam's banger-senses tingling. Or, to be more precise, it was what was *below* the balcony.

'Nuh-uh,' said Callum. 'No way.'

'Pleeeeeeaaaase?' Adam begged as he dropped to his knees with puppy-dog eyes and praying hands. 'It'll look so cool!'

'Then *you* do it!'

'But it makes such a better title if you do it,' Adam reasoned. '"*I Made My Little Brother Jump into the Pool from the First-Floor Balcony*" is so much cooler than "*I Made Myself Jump into the Pool from the First-Floor Balcony*."'

'Yeah, and "*I Made Myself Jump into the Pool from the First-Floor Balcony*" is so much cooler than "*I Made My Awesome Little Brother Die by Forcing Him to Do a Stupid Stunt for One of My Stupid Videos Because I'm a Stupid, Stupid-Head*."'

'Aww, come on, Cal!' he pleaded. 'It could really help my channel! Jumping from great heights, little kids in peril ... everyone LOVES that stuff!'

'No, not everyone loves that stuff,' Callum corrected him. 'The little kids in peril HATE IT! I, your little brother who is afraid of heights, HATES IT.'

Adam got the feeling that Callum wasn't really up for it.

So he would just have to do the jump himself. It was no big deal. The balcony was no higher than the diving board at their local pool.

All he would have to do was climb over the railing of the balcony and take a leap. A big leap. A leap big enough for him to reach the pool without catching himself on the concrete edge directly below the balcony.

Actually, the more he thought about it, the more

it freaked him out – *What if I don't jump far enough? What if I hit the edge of the pool with my foot? Or my butt? Or my head? What if I miss the pool completely?* No, Adam decided, just to be safe, he was going to have to take a run-up.

So, while Mum and Callum were downstairs, drinking breakfast mocktails in the sauna, he set up all his cameras around the pool, he got into his trunks and he prepared himself for the second-biggest stunt of his life.

At the far end of his room, Adam readied himself for action. He crouched down like a sprinter at the starting blocks. He took a long, controlled breath. Then another. Then a third. And then … *he was off.* He darted across the room, powering himself forwards with every step. He zoomed towards the open window, readied himself to leap over the balcony, and then –

'WHAT AM I DOING?!'

The sheer never-should-have-considered-this-in-a-million-years stupidity of the whole enterprise suddenly hit him like a custard pie to the face.

'WHAT IF THE POOL'S NOT DEEP ENOUGH! I'LL

SHATTER MY HEAD! AND MY BOTTOM! AND ALL MY BONES!'

Fearing for his life, Adam slammed on the brakes, bailing out at the last minute. But he was going too fast! He couldn't stop! And when he hit the balcony, he was still rocketing forwards. He wasn't going fast enough to launch himself at the pool, but he wasn't going slowly enough to stop himself from lurching over the other side!

Over he went. Spinning ... screaming ... plummeting ... headfirst. Straight towards the concrete.

Adam's body spun out of control. The entire world was a tumbling blur. He knew that he was moments away from agony. Or death. Or at least a whole lot of shouting from Mum. And there was nothing he could do to stop it.

Panic struck him like a bolt of lightning.

His vision flashed white.

A jolt of electricity kicked him in the brain.

His vision flashed white again.

A deafening screech tore at his ears.

A third flash! But ... wait ... was it his vision? Or did those flashes actually come from the screens of the cameras filming him?

As he fell, time almost seemed to slow down.

The ground wasn't racing towards him as fast as he'd expected.

The whole thing seemed to happen in ... *slow motion*.

Things were slow enough for him to take a good look around ... Slow enough to notice that he was still level with the balcony ... Slow enough to be able to reach his right leg out and kick off from the balcony ledge, pushing himself further out towards the pool, away from the concrete below.

What is going ON here? Adam asked himself as he tumbled into an astronaut-like slow-motion somersault until he was just half a metre above the pool. *Popularis? Are* you *doing thi——?*

WHOOOOSH!

Time sped back up.

Adam plummeted downwards, and ...

SPLASH!

He plopped straight into the centre of the pool, light years away from any of the edges. No

spine-breaking agony. No death. No shouting. Just pure relief, a mountain of gratitude and a head full of confusion.

20

GBFPAPFFNSWBAERRD

There was a crash from the kitchen as Mum dropped a saucepan and came running outside.

It looked like there might be just the teensiest bit of shouting after all.

'What happened?! What was it?' she gasped in panic. 'I heard a little girl screaming! Then a massive splash! Adam, what is going on?!'

Adam made his eyes as wide as golf balls and did his best to look innocent, surprised and shocked, all at once.

'What? No! Nothing! Nope! Hmm?'

'Adam, you're as white as a sheet. Are sure you're OK?'

'Yes! No! I mean yes! Nothing! I'm fine! Just …

you know, relaxing. And swimming. And singing.
Perhaps that's what you heard – *LAAAAAAAAA!* –
maybe?'

'Well, you'd better stop now and go and see why
that man at the gate is trying to get your attention.
You haven't made any plans for us that I should
know about, have you?'

Adam turned to see a cheerful taxi driver waving
frantically from the villa gates, then turned back
to Mum.

'Ah,' he said awkwardly. 'About that. Well, you
see … We may need to get ready for a day out. A
very *big* day out. Very quickly. Right *now*.'

Adam shuddered out a deep breath as Mum
rushed back inside to get ready. He didn't have time
to flip out about the unbelievable oddity of how
he had just fallen into the pool in slow motion. He
would have to put off feeling traumatised for later,
because he had far too many other things to think
about first.

Like his million-and-one plans for the entire rest
of the day, otherwise known as the GREAT BIG,
FAST-PACED, ACTION-PACKED, FUN-FUELLED,

NON-STOP, WHAM-BAM-ALAKAZZAM, EPIC ROLLER-COASTER RIDE OF A DAY! (Or GBFPAPFFNSWBAERRD for short.)

First stop for GBFPAPFFNSWBAERRD was the beach, where the three of them had an all-out, top-speed, high-octane, guns-blazing water pistol fight while riding jet skis. The end result was a video that could be perfectly described with just four words – *BRRRRRM!* – *SQUIRT!* – *'AAARRGHHH!'* – *SPLASH!* (Mum surprised them all by being the hands-down champion of this game.)

Next up was 'Ninja Beach Warrior' – where they had to leap, climb and scramble their way across a series of inflatable hurdles all put together to make a near-impossible obstacle course in the sea. In four words – *LEAP* – *SLIP* – *'NOOOOOO!'* – *SPLOOSH!* (Mum surprised no one by having a bash at the first obstacle, then refusing to do any more.)

And finally, Adam had saved the biggest of the three 'GBFPAPFFNSWBAERRD' videos till last – *SKYDIVING!* Which, as you probably already know, involves leaping out of a plane, then falling towards the ground at one hundred and twenty-five miles per hour (usually strapped to a qualified instructor named Bret or Taz or Zara). In four words – '*AAAARRGHHHHH!*' – '*AAAARRGHHHHH!*' – '*AAAARRGHHHHH!*' – '*AAAARRGHHHHH!*' (Mum surprised them all, again, by actually agreeing to do it! And then she unsurprised them by chickening out. And then she re-surprised them by changing her mind. And then she re-unsurprised them by bottling out again. And then her instructor, Faz, suggested she watched from the ground, with a cup of tea and a slice of cake, and they were all quite relieved.) And it turned out Callum was too young to do it anyway. Which just left Adam to do it by himself.

He did a good impression of being confident. He laughed, he bounced up and down, he clapped his hands, and thennnnn … he passed out for the entire jump. At first he was disappointed. Like, 'The entire jump was completely wasted!' levels of disappointment. But then he played the video back and realised that watching himself fall thousands of feet with his tongue lolling out of his mouth, while strapped to a huge bearded man named Zook, was way more entertaining than watching someone with their eyes *open* and their tongue *inside* their mouth repeatedly shouting, 'WOOOHOOOOO! WOOOH! YEAH! WOOOOHOOO! YEEAAAAHHH!'

By the time they got back to the villa, they were all so tired they could hardly move, *especially* Adam. But, as exhausted as he was, he was way too excited about editing the videos to even *think* about going to bed. He quickly scanned through some of the day's highlights and felt his pulse racing at how amazing it all looked.

Then he reached his 'Balcony Jump' footage and his jaw *really* hit the floor.

Adam must have watched the video back at least one hundred times and he still couldn't make sense of it. It had captured everything – the run-up, the jump, the tripping over the balcony, the slo-mo fall, the safe landing – it even caught him scrambling out of the pool, retching for breath, then throwing up in a towel when Mum wasn't looking. It wasn't just the fear of the fall that had brought on the *bleurghh*, it was the experience of being completely and utterly under the control of an inexplicable force that Adam could only assume was …

KNOCK KNOCK!

'Adam, sweetie, dinner will be ready in half an hour,' his mum said gently at the doorway. 'And, I know you've got one more video planned for today, but can it *please* be something that doesn't involve enormous amounts of physical activity? Like, just pigging out on the sofa? Today was *far* too much fun for my weary old bones!'

'Mum, trust me, my next video is going to be *sooo* relaxing. Have you ever heard of base jumping?'

'Adam, no!' Mum turned white.

'I'm joking!' Adam laughed. 'How about we just watch a film?'

'Now *that* I can manage! Let's do it!'

'I'll be down in half an hour,' Adam smiled, throwing a kiss through the air to her. Then, just as she was leaving – 'Hey, Mum, can I just show you something?'

The balcony video was too much for Adam to keep to himself. He *had* to show someone, to talk about it, to marvel at its epic-ness.

His mum looked as if she was about to say something along the lines of *'Now? It's so late. Can it wait until tomorrow?'* but Adam beat her to it.

'Actually, don't worry, I'll show you tomorrow when I've edited it. It'll look even more impressive then.'

As desperate as he was to talk about it, something told him Mum wasn't the person for the job. Just like everyone who saw the bike stunt; she would assume he'd used some kind of video trickery to make it look as though he'd slowed down in mid-air. Rather than marvel at its amazingness, she'd be likely to give him a massive telling-off for trying something as idiotic as jumping from a balcony. There's no way she'd believe it was magic. There's no way *anyone* would believe it was magic. Except one person – one *thing* – the thing responsible for the stunt in the first place.

'It was you, wasn't it, Popularis?' Adam whispered at his laptop once Mum had gone. 'And it *was* magic, wasn't it? You did it to help me. You saw that I was in danger, and you *saved* me, just like you did with the bike stunt in the park. That was you, too, I *know* it was. You made my camera screen do that blinding flash-y thing both times. You're on my side. So ... what was the WebCon thing about? Humiliating me onstage like that? That wasn't nice. It doesn't seem like the kind of thing you would do.'

And then Adam thought about it. There had been no blinding flashes before the Nappy-rena video at WebCon; no deafening screeches tearing at his ears. The reason it didn't seem like the kind of thing Popularis would do was because it *wasn't* Popularis!

But if it wasn't Popularis, that meant it was somebody else. Was somebody out to get him?

But who? Adam wondered. *Who would do a thing like that? And WHY?*

The shock almost made him feel like his old shy, bullied, School Adam-self. But he didn't let it. He *wasn't* School Adam anymore. And it *wasn't* Popularis who had humiliated him at WebCon. Which meant Popularis was *definitely* on his side. He had *magic* on his side! Sure, it was magic that only appeared when it chose to — Adam had no control over it — but it was helping him all the same. Helping him with his videos, helping him make decisions, helping him out of *mortal danger*. Even if somebody *was* out to get him, thanks to Popularis he suddenly felt a tiny bit invincible. *Unstoppable*.

And with electric excitement buzzing through his veins, Adam began preparing for his *next* video. It was waiting to be filmed downstairs. It would be the simplest, shortest, nothing-est video of the day – and it would be the biggest hit of the holiday.

21

Unbearable Fun

There was something about Adam's plan for the day's final video that caused a sneaky, cheeky smirk to creep across his sly little face every time he thought about it. The smirk had first appeared when Callum came shuffling downstairs for breakfast, dragging his new giant bear with him. The smirk was still there when the oversized toy joined them at the pool, on its very own sun lounger.

But when they settled down for the evening, to watch a film in the cinema room (yes, they had a *cinema room*!), Adam's smirk was nowhere to be seen ... mainly because *Adam* was nowhere to be seen. It was just Callum on one sofa, Mum on another and the giant bear, flopped on a gigantic beanbag in the corner of the room, waiting for Adam to join them.

'Adam!' Mum called.

They waited …

'Come onnnn!' groaned Callum.

And they waited …

'Adam, where are you?!'

And they waited …

But there was no sign of him. And that's because he had unstitched the back of the bear, pulled half the stuffing out, climbed inside it, then flopped himself on the beanbag, and hadn't moved a muscle for a full twenty minutes. Adam was in the very same room as them. And so was his cheeky, sneaky smirk.

'Adam! Come on! Or we'll put the film on without you!' Callum bellowed.

'Ughhh!' Mum complained, before prising herself from her comfortable seat and marching out of the room to find him.

It was just Callum and the bear now.

Callum picked his nose.

Adam watched in frozen silence.

Callum ate a handful of popcorn.

Adam made a mental note not to eat any of that popcorn.

Callum picked his nose some more.

And then ...

'BRRRAAAAAARRRGHHHHHHHH!'

The toy bear leaped off the beanbag!

It launched itself at Callum!

Callum gave a scream to shatter bulletproof glass!

The entire bucket of popcorn went up in the air!

The bear charged at him, claws bared!

And then Callum raised the pool cue that he had been inexplicably holding and began swinging it around in giant arcs like it was a katana.

Adam had *not* been expecting this, and, as a result, *he* let loose a series of screams to shatter bulletproof glass as he ducked and ducked and ducked some more.

Then Callum tripped over the sofa and went toppling over the back of it.

This made Adam laugh so hard that ... well, let's

just say that having its back torn open and its insides removed was not the worst thing to happen to the toy bear that day.

Twenty minutes later, once the laughter had subsided, the adrenalin had dissipated and the film had sent Mum and Callum to sleep, Adam pressed pause and darted up to his room to continue editing all five of the day's videos.

His phone, which had run out of battery four

times that day, was on the bed, charging, with half a million unread messages lighting up the screen (OK, more like ten or twenty messages, but it *seemed* like half a million).

18:20 from Bruce K:

> Man, can't wait to see some new vids hope you're having a banging time

18:43 from Ethan:

Can't believe you're off having fun in the sun and you've left me here! Boringest! Day! Ever!

19:38 from Bruce:

Adam search for best videos of all time and your bike stunt crops up in nearly every list!

20:03 from Ethan:

Picked up your science homework. Don't say I never do anything for you x

20:03 from Ethan:

Ignore the kiss! It was an accident! So used to putting them on for Mum and Dad! X

20:03 from Ethan:

Gah! And again! No kisses this time, promise (just a hug) o

There was something weird going on inside Adam, and when he eventually put his finger on what it was his little mind was completely blown.

'Is it true?' he whispered to his phone. 'Is Bruce actually becoming a *better friend than Ethan*?!'

Adam used to find it completely unbelievable when his mum would talk about how his dad and Stan Kilter used to work together on Dad's computer research. Apparently, as toddlers, he and Bruce even used to have play dates together. The idea of him and Bruce ever being friends had always been like trying to imagine hot snow, or strawberry-scented farts — it was *impossible*. But now … ? Adam's brain was slowly coming round to the idea that Bruce wasn't as bad as he pretended to be.

The person who had been singlehandedly responsible for making so many years of Adam's life completely and utterly miserable was now proving to be the person singlehandedly making Adam feel *better* about himself.

Am I right? he wondered to himself. *Do I really prefer Bruce to Ethan?*

The next two messages seemed to answer that question. First ...

20:58 from Bruce:

WHOA! Man half a mil! Congrats!

Adam's heart skipped a beat when he saw what accompanied the message – a three-second screenshot of the exact moment Adam's subs had rolled over from 499k to 500k, less than two hours ago.

'WHOA!' Adam gasped. 'I'm halfway there!' He leaped from his chair and was tempted to run back downstairs to wake Mum and Callum up, and dance them around the cinema room, singing, 'Haaaaaaalf ... way! Halfway! Halfway, halfway, halfway!'

Another message pinged through and Adam wondered if it was Ethan telling him exactly the same news.

22:38 from Ethan:

> Adam! How did I not notice this! It's
> amazing! I can't believe it! Vimto is
> an anagram of VOMIT! Seriously!
> And that totally makes sense, right?
> Because if you make it too strong it
> actually TASTES like vomit. Makes you
> wonder if they did it on purpose.

Oh. Not quite. Still, Adam was buzzing so much from the 500k news that he could not stop smiling. He was halfway to reaching his goal, and he wasn't even five months into his twelve-month deadline!

With this news, plus his five HUGE new videos, Adam could finally feel those Mentos beginning to bubble up in his Coke bottle of life!

And then came another message from Ethan:

22:40 from Ethan:

> Has YT gone haywire, or is it you that's had
> a breakdown?

Adam had to reply. The message made no sense, but he was intrigued.

22:40 from Adam:

Huh?

22:40 from Ethan:

Your channel is disappearing right in front of me, one video at a time!

Adam was sure it would be a problem that only existed on Ethan's unreliable PC, but, just like when someone tells you your flies are undone, he had to check. He marched over to his desk, opened his laptop and twelve seconds later he was trembling from head to toe. Every video he'd uploaded in the past six weeks was gone. Vanished completely. Disappeared without a trace, as though they'd never even been there.

But how? *And why now?!* Had someone stolen his

password? Hacked his account? Installed malware? Cloned his computer?

But Adam was always so careful when it came to security!

He'd already made his mind up that his magical assistant was on his side, so that ruled Popularis out of the equation. But who else could have done this? Sure, Ethan knew his password, but he'd had it ever since the #Slimeboy video. He wouldn't do something like that, Adam was sure of it.

It was *way* too stupid to be a Callum prank. It was almost the exact *opposite* to what Bruce would do these days.

Adam couldn't figure it out. And until he did, he wouldn't know how to fix it! And he desperately had to fix it – his entire channel was being deleted, one video at a time!

Hang on – the villa. Adam had been so excited that he hadn't bothered to check that the Wi-Fi was secure. Someone could have been intercepting his data every time he went online!

A local Ibiza hacker? Adam wondered. *Or is someone out specifically to sabotage me? Has someone snuck past my web security to undo all of my hard work, like some Trojan Assassin? A Trojan idiot?!*

With a sudden unshakeable clarity, Adam knew that whoever had been responsible for his Nappy-rena humiliation was also responsible for this.

Adam sent a frenzied email to YouTube, explaining that he had been hacked. Then he slammed his laptop shut and didn't dare open it again. He had to fix this. *Fast*. And there was only one place he knew was safe to do it.

'Mum! Callum!' he yelled as he raced down the stairs. 'Wake up! And pack your bags. We've got to go home. *Right now!*'

22

Bigger than Huge

Adam was in a meeting. A very serious meeting.
And Adam's knees were trembling because …

'I'm so thrilled we're doing this, Adam!' said the
tall, blond, very serious Irishman sitting opposite
him as he closed his very serious laptop.

Adam was feeling sick because …

'OK, so, that's for you, aaaaand … so is that,'
said the tall, blond, very serious Irishman, handing
Adam two very serious stacks of paper. 'If you just
sign those and send them back to us, once you've
read them.'

Adam felt like he was going to *faint* because …

'THIS IS THE MOST EXCITING THING I'VE
EVER HEARD IN MY ENTIRE LIFE!' Adam

blurted so loudly that the very serious Irishman almost spilt his entire coffee down his very serious shirt. 'Sorry,' added Adam with a splutter of nervous laughter.

When the tall, blond, very serious Irishman (or Chris for short) had first emailed Adam, asking if he was free for a meeting in a local coffee shop – *this* meeting – Adam had shrieked with excitement because Chris, it turns out, was a big-time agent with the world's number-one agency for Creators – Studio Cre8. When, during their coffee shop meeting, Chris had asked Adam if he would like to sign with their agency, Adam shrieked with excitement, slapped his cheeks in amazement, then said, 'Sorry, I mean, *yes! Of course! Please!*' And when Chris had told Adam that he had some exciting news to share with him, then gave just the *tiniest hint* of what that exciting news was, Adam shrieked with excitement, slapped his cheeks in amazement, then began singing, dancing, jumping, whooping, clapping, spinning, running, squealing, gasping and 'Oh-my-life-ing' all over the shop (except he managed to do all of this inside his head while, on the outside, he remained perfectly composed. Completely silent. He didn't move a single muscle. He was the ultimate professional. Until a tiny little 'woooo!' escaped his lips, and he had to pretend it was a sneeze. Which was a bit weird).

And then Chris went on to explain in full, glorious detail exactly what this 'exciting idea' was, and Adam couldn't take it any longer – the excitement was too much. That's when something in Adam's brain popped, and the trembling knees, feeling sick, fainting stuff all began.

But somehow, by some inexplicable miracle, Adam continued to hold his explosive excitement in. He managed to shake Chris's hand 'goodbye' without hugging him or spinning him in circles and singing with joy. He managed to walk all the way to the coffee shop exit without leaping on any of the tables, or high-fiving any of the other customers, or doing strange screaming or dancing of any kind!

'Oh, Adam?' Chris called as Adam was almost out of the door. 'You said you had some problems with YouTube. Hackers, or something?'

'Oh, that's all sorted. YouTube reversed it all for

me. I changed my passwords, got new security software, got a *new phone*,' Adam assured him, waving his brand-new, top-of-the-range, way-better-than-Bruce's phone in the air as though this was somehow going to make Chris yelp with excitement.

But, if Adam was completely honest, there was still a buzz of fear constantly knocking against the inside of his skull, like a bee trapped in a jar, whispering its worries to him all day long – *What if the Trojan Idiot returns? What if they're not gone at all? What if they come back and ruin more things? What if they come back and ruin THIS?! How can you stop them if you don't know who they are?*

'Fantastic.' Chris smiled and gave a thumbs up. 'So no more internet weirdness?'

'Err … nope! Definitely not!'

This was possibly the biggest lie Adam had ever told. Internet weirdness was definitely *not* over. Internet weirdness was his life. Dancing in nappies, being guided by a magical internet wizard, being sabotaged by a Trojan Idiot cyber attacker … there was *nothing but* internet weirdness!

'It's all good then?' Chris pressed.

'One hundred per cent.' Adam nodded.

'Great stuff. "One hundred per cent" certain is absolutely what we need to be before October. October is going to be *big*, Adam. Scratch that – it's going to be *MASSIVE*! And you really don't want any gremlins in the works, messing things up for you.'

Just the thought of anything messing this news up made Adam feel instantly sick. You see, the tall blond Chris was wrong. October wasn't going to be massive. It was going to be bigger than massive – it was going to be *gigantic*! No, it was going to be *GARGANTUAN*! (If gargantuan is bigger than gigantic. Come to think of it, is gigantic definitely bigger than massive? Let's just play it safe and say that October was going to be *EPICALLY GIMANTUAN*!)

So Adam pushed his worries aside. He put the lid back on the jar inside his head that contained the buzzing bee of worry, and he reminded himself that while he had *magic* on his side, he was absolutely unstoppable. Worry took a step back, and another emotion quickly jumped in to take its place –

pure twenty-four-carat-gold *excitement!*

The news that Chris had given him was too much to contain!

Adam felt like a volcano ready to erupt with joy!

He managed to drag his trembling, quivering, buzzing-with-10,000-volts-of-gleeful-disbelief body out of the coffee shop, all the way around the corner, on to the next street, and then he couldn't hold it in any longer –

'WAHOOOOOOOOOOOOO!!!' he screamed at the top of his lungs as he aeroplaned down the busy pavement, laughing and running and cheering and skipping and whooping and spinning and high-fiving every stranger that didn't run away from him, until he reached Café de la Food, where Mum and Callum were waiting for him, and he burst inside and announced 'OCTOBER! *YESSSS!*'

'*Whoa!*' shrieked Mum, Callum and every single other person in Café de la Food, all jumping back as if Adam might literally explode at any moment.

'What's *wrong* with you?' Mum whisper-screamed.

'OCTOBER!' Adam repeated with a spin and a jump and a clap and a squeal.

'*SHHHHHHH! Sit down!* What about October?' asked his mum, wild with confusion and pink with embarrassment.

But Adam was too electrified to *shhhhhh* or sit down or even string a sentence together. So he explained in the best way he could – by grabbing Mum by the hands and dancing her round in circles, while singing, 'OHHHHHHH … MYYYYYY … LIFE! MY LIFE! MY LIFE, MY LIFE MY LIFE …'

'Explain!' his mum demanded, forcing Adam out of the café, into the street, followed by Callum as she tried to wipe her mascara, which was streaming down her face from laughing so hard.

'GUYS!' Adam squealed at Mum and Callum as he grabbed them by the shoulders. 'I CAN'T BELIEVE IT!'

'Can't believe *what*?' Mum and Callum shouted together, not able to stand the anticipation any longer.

'IT'S GOING TO BE *GIMANTUAN*!'

'*WHAT IS?!*'

'GUYS ... THEY WANT ME TO DO A SHOW!'

'A what?'

'A *LIVE* SHOW!'

'A *what?*'

'AT THE *LONDON ARENA!*'

And the squealing and spinning and clapping and whooping and cheering and dancing continued, right there in the street, times three.

23

Sensilly

BOOM! If Adam's life was a bottle of Coke, then this London Arena news was definitely the metaphorical Mentos. His life was finally beginning to feel fizzy. His five holiday videos were the biggest hits his channel had seen all year, and at 542k, his subs were finally creeping up again.

Adam should have known that something good would turn up again. It was just like his dad had once said – 'Everything is temporary, Adam. The good times are temporary, so don't take them for granted. The bad times are temporary, so don't stress yourself about them too much. And *life* is temporary, Adam, so make sure you make every second of it count!'

Even with *his* luck, which seemed to go up and down like a yo-yo, Adam could never have expected just how gimantuanly 'up' this new 'up' would be. As soon as his next YouTube payment came through, he celebrated by buying himself a TV for his bedroom (well, *he* called it a TV. Mum and Callum called it a 'cinema screen' it was so big – bigger than the one in their hotel room at WebCon. Even bigger than the one he'd seen in Bruce's video message!). He had made a mental plan for Mum's new car that allowed him to '*spend now, reward later*' as he put it.

Taking small bites out of the fund wasn't an issue any more, because not only was this plan brilliant, it was also quite possible that it would provide Adam with the biggest banger of his career!

It was simple; bangers always are. After the London show he'd have the car waiting in the loading bay and present it to Mum. Emotions would be high that night anyway, but this, *this* would push happy tears into the stratosphere (and make for one heck of a video!).

So, for now the extremely large TV stayed in his

room, completely guilt-free. The only problem was …
Adam could not bring himself to fix it to the wall.

Not because he didn't know *how*, but because
when he went to get the drill and the screwdriver
he couldn't even bring himself to pick them up.
Those were Dad's tools, Dad's jobs, they were indisputable 'Dad things' and they were sacred. To take
them up and use them without permission, as
though they were his own, felt like the ultimate
betrayal of his memory. It felt like saying, 'Thanks,
Dad, but we don't need you any more. Consider
yourself replaced.'

So not only did Adam refuse to do any 'Dad
things' in the house, he also couldn't bear to see
anyone else do any of those 'Dad things', which was
why no one had done any 'crazy leg dancing' to
Stevie Wonder while cooking dinner. It was why
they had gone for a real Christmas tree last year,
because Dad was always the one who assembled the
fake one; it was why no one raced as Baby Peach in
Mario Kart; it was why no one had uttered the words
'love you one million' since he'd gone; it was why
no one had been tickled until they almost wet them-

selves; and it was why the house was literally crawling with un-caught spiders.

But there were grown-up things that Adam found he *could* do, things that he'd never seen Dad do, things he never knew he was capable of, like having Zoom meetings with professional grown-up Studio Cre8 executives. It was a bizarre new life for Adam. In the morning he'd be hiding in the cereal cupboard to scare Callum, and in the afternoon he'd be discussing 'the average age of his fan base' with the Studio Cre8 marketing director. Just that Monday he'd spent all day on a bouncy castle covered in foam, on Tuesday he was in a boardroom with six members of the Studio Cre8 creative development team. On Friday morning, he was discussing rehearsal schedules with a lady named Constance, and in the evening he was flooding his kitchen with frothy brown liquid. With each and every day, he found that he became a little bit ... Actually, no, sorry, let's go back to that bit about the frothy liquid. It's way too good to just skim over ...

You see, since Adam had mastered the art of dropping metaphorical Mentos into his metaphorical Coke bottle of life, he decided that now was the time he should try it for real – *real* Mentos, *real* Coke, *real* life. *Callum's* real life, to be specific.

Well, that was the plan, at least.

- 4 hidden cameras (including one actually *inside* the fridge)
- 1 bottle of Coke
- 2 Mentos
- 1 piece of cotton, threaded through the Mentos and twisted into the lid, just dangling there, waiting to create frothy brown anarchy
- One Friday night, 12:04 a.m.
- 2.8 million views

And the video went something like this –

A pair of bare feet tiptoe into the dark kitchen, then are suddenly flooded with light when the fridge door is opened. Cut to the fridge cam, which reveals, not Callum, but MUM rooting through the chilled goods for a late-night snack. First she plucks a handful of grapes from their packet and pops them in her mouth, next she takes a quick bite from the corner of a block of cheese, and then it finally happens – she spots the bottle of Coke just waiting in the fridge door, begging for someone to drink it. She picks the bottle up, holds it tight to her chest as she begins to unscrew the lid ...

The thread drops ...

The Mentos plummet ...

A minor earthquake rumbles in the bottom of the bottle, and then ...

SPLOOOOOSH! An entire litre of Coke shoots up into her face! It blows her hair back! It jet-washes both her nostrils! Then it sends her flailing to the floor in a sugary puddle of bubbly badness, and a scream rings out across the entire neighbourhood – 'ADAAAAAAAAAAAAAAAMMMMM!'

Nine hours later, Adam was in a Zoom meeting in the living room, wearing a freshly ironed shirt and a very sensible face, discussing health and safety with a roomful of Studio Cre8 serious-types.

Does that give you a sense of the balancing act Adam was performing? One minute he was the most sensible human on the planet, the next minute he was the silliest. And it was a skill he had mastered

to a tee. He was so good at it that Callum declared him the King of Sensilly (sensible and silly mixed together). He was up and down like a yo-yo in a lift. It was like riding on a see-saw by himself, and he had figured out a way of rocking both ends. But every now and then something came along to ruin that momentum. Little things. Annoying, time-wasting, pestering things. Mainly school. And homework. And chores. And sleep. And speaking of annoying, time-wasting, pestering things –

'What are you doing in my room, you little Bean Head?!' barked Adam, returning from a particularly boring meeting to find Callum sitting on his bed.

'I was keeping Ethan company while he waited for you,' explained Callum, with his big 'don't be cross at me!' puppy-dog eyes.

Adam turned around and was shocked to see Ethan sitting right there at his computer, his hand hovering over the keyboard. It felt weird to see Ethan in his room again, touching his things. It felt ... *wrong*. Not so long ago, Ethan would come round every single day after school. But this was the first time he'd been round in *months*.

'Ethan! How long have you been here? If I'd known you were coming, I'd have tidied up!'

And maybe locked my computer! he thought. *What were you doing with your hand on it anyway?*

'Yeah, I was passing by,' explained Ethan. 'So I thought I'd drop in, you know, see if you'd bought yourself the biggest TV ever made, or ... Oh, look! You did! Weird! And, like, well, I thought it'd be nice to hang out a bit, like old times. Or, like, maybe I could help with your videos or something. I don't know, like ... yeah.'

'That'd be really cool, but I've got, like, three videos to edit, so ...' Adam gave a shrug and a wince, then finished with – 'sorry. But maybe some other time?'

'Definitely!' agreed Ethan. 'OK, well, I guess I'll see you at school.'

As they said goodbye, and Ethan showed himself out, there was an unignorable weirdness in the air. It was not like old times one little bit. But Adam didn't have time to think about it. He really did have three videos to edit, and he was running out of time, so it really wasn't a good moment for—

KNOCK! KNOCK!

'Adam, I know you're busy, but are you OK to help me with this bit of homework? Only Mum's never home, and I've got to get it in by—'

'OH MY LIFE! WHY CAN'T PEOPLE JUST LEAVE ME ALONE?!'

'Sorry,' muttered Callum, quietly backing out of the room.

PING!

18:25 from Bruce:

> *Every single video you've uploaded has been a belter! How do you do it? Just don't work yourself too hard.*
> *Mucho respect*

'Finally!' Adam roared with relief as he read Bruce's message. 'Someone actually *gets* me!'

18:25 from Adam:

THANK YOU!
You've hit the nail on the head!
Working SO hard you wouldn't
believe it!

18:26 from Bruce:

Just don't forget to PLAY
as well as work, mate!

18:26 from Adam:

PLAY? I wish!
No such luck right now.
BIG things are happening!

18:26 from Bruce:

NOOOOO! You can't just put
that out there and leave me
hangin! WHAT big things?

Adam had already made his mind up not to tell anyone else about his London show for now. Not until he'd made his big reveal in a video. But, right then, he felt like he really *needed* to tell someone. It would be a weight off his mind. And since Bruce was the only person who seemed to be listening ...

18:29 from Adam:

> OK.
> Promise you won't
> tell a living soul?

18:29 from Bruce:

> Mate. Word is bond.

21:30 from Adam:

> See you at registration
> tomorrow, be early!

Adam had no idea what 'word is bond' meant, but he guessed it meant something like 'cross my heart and hope to die', so he went ahead and met with Bruce the next morning at school.

'C'mon then, spill. I could barely sleep!' Bruce slid into his seat at the back of the class like a covert operative working for the CIA. Or the FBI. Or … *you get the picture*!

'Right, so, I had a meeting a few days ago with that Chris guy …' Adam's eyes shifted as he spoke. 'And he wants to be my agent …'

'Right? OK? That's very cool. And … ?'

'Well …'

'Spit it out, man!' Bruce giggled.

'I'm doing a live show at the London Arena!' Adam scanned every fibre of Bruce's being waiting for a response. And when it came, it was worth it.

'WHAT!'

'*SSSHHHH!*'

'Sorry …' That word still sounded completely alien coming out of Bruce Kilter's mouth. 'This is bigger than massive. You know what, I'm proud of you, I mean that! The London Arena!'

Adam hadn't expected Bruce to be that excited – with all his family's money, everything in Bruce's life always seemed so much bigger and better than in his – but Bruce continued to flip for the next nine-and-a-half minutes.

'Hey, what's so exciting?' asked Ethan, sidling up to the giggling duo and eyeing Bruce nervously.

'What have I missed?'

'Hang on, Ethan,' said Adam as Bruce laid a celebratory high-five on him that transitioned into a secret handshake. 'I'll tell you later.'

Adam glanced at Ethan as he quietly made his way back to his seat, and thought about he'd had said the other day about helping Adam make videos. It wasn't actually a bad idea.

Adam was so busy with his Studio Cre8, London Arena show stuff, he could really do with some extra help.

'So, Bruce, anyway, I was wondering … you wanna help make a few vids sometime?'

Bruce looked back at Adam with a dazzling smile.

'You're on, my friend!'

24

Busy

I *might as well get this over with*, Adam thought, and pulled his phone from his pocket.

Telling Bruce about the show had given him the little boost of positivity he needed. He was about to pull the pin from the YouTube grenade and hopefully create a BANG(er)!

As soon as Adam clicked 'upload video' his heart began to race. He was finally letting people know that he was doing a *live show at the London Arena* and it somehow made it seem more real. More terrifying. More exciting.

Adam slid his phone away, then leaned over to confide in his buddy once again.

'Bruce, that's not all.'

Bruce moved in close to hear properly.

'I'm giving my mum a new car after the show. I've got the whole thing planned out to perfection. Picture it – me, Mum and Callum are on our way out of the hotel. There's a car waiting outside. Mum's all, like, "Oooooh!" and "F-A-N-C-Y! Another space rocket ride to the airport!" Then I say – "That's no taxi, Mum. It's YOUR NEW CAR!" And I hand her the keys, and she's all, like, laughing and crying and "You're the best son in the world!" and then we drive it all the way back to Derry, and we make a proper road trip of it, and it's going to be *immense*!'

'Wow!' laughed Bruce. 'I never knew anyone could get so excited about a *car*!'

Yeah, that's because you've got about fifty, and we've got none! Adam almost said out loud.

'I've ordered it and everything,' Adam continued. 'I pay half now, and the rest the day before the show. I can't *wait*!'

But there was a part of him that *could* wait. A part of him that was panicking beyond belief. A part of him that was harbouring a secret he hoped no one else – especially Chris and the guys at Studio Cre8 – had spotted …

Nobody was watching his videos!

Adam had hoped that it was just a temporary setback – sometimes viewer numbers go up and down for no real reason – but this wasn't just a little drop in views. It was a *beyond gimantuan* drop, because literally *nobody* new was coming to watch *anything* he uploaded! The comments had gone from thousands a day, to just two –

- **ginglepopper266** 'I am SO confsd right now? Why is nobody else watching this chnl? It is THE BEST CHNL EVER! I LOVE YOU ADAM!!' 👍 2 👎
- **LordStarDwarf992** 'True to the max @**ginglepopper266** I was thinking same. Where is everyone? Something weird going on here, right?' 👍 1 👎

Adam had to agree. Something weird was DEFINITELY going on …

He was beginning to suspect *The Return of the Trojan idiot*, or even *The Saboteur Strikes Back*.

At any other time those Star Wars references

would have caused Adam to chuckle at himself. Not today, though. This was real, and this was scary.

If this *was* the work of the Trojan Idiot, how were they doing it? How could someone or something cause thousands of people to *not* watch your videos? It seemed like some kind of dark magic.

And then an even scarier thought occurred to him. *What if it's NOT the Trojan Idiot? What if people are just bored of me? What if I've peaked and no one wants to watch me any more? What if I never make enough money to pay for the rest of Mum's car? What if the London Arena cancels my show because no one buys any tickets? What if I don't get to one million? What if I lose all I hold dear? My channel might be gone forever!*

Panic was eating him alive. But no, Adam wouldn't let himself believe it. He *knew*, beyond any doubt, for absolute sure, that his big 'I'm Doing a Live Show at the London Arena!' reveal would turn things around. He knew it would get people watching him again, get people talking about him more, get his subs to grow once again.

And the next day, when he checked his subs, his eyes almost popped out of their sockets.

25

The Big Subs Boost

It was officially the first day of the summer holidays.

The numbers on Adam's clock read 1:12 – one hundred and twelve days until his time was up. One hundred and *eleven* days until his live show.

And the views for Adam's latest video – 'My Biggest Reveal EVER!' – were at a grand total of ...

0
(Well, not quite, but 156 did feel like zero!)

Adam's subs had grown by a grand total of zero.

Adam's panic was at a grand total of *one hundred per cent*.

It didn't make sense! He had copied the video format, note for note, from Ed Almighty's 'I'm Touring the UK' reveal, which had been a massive hit for him! So why had it gone so badly wrong for Adam?

It didn't matter. He knew there was one sure way to fix it.

'Popularis? I need your help!'

Adam thanked his lucky stars that, when it came to terrifyingly impossible life hurdles like this, he had Popularis watching his back. Except, there seemed to be one tiny hitch – Popularis was missing in action once more.

'Popularis? Come on, man, this isn't funny. You can't just bail on me like this.'

Adam had spent hours typing, scouring the internet, warbling 'Hell-*ooo*-ooo?' at every vaguely screen-like object in the house (including the microwave door) and trying to communicate using only the power of his mind, but not a single thing was working.

'Popularis! This is *serious*! You can't do this to me! Did Aladdin's genie just quit after two wishes? Did Cinderella's fairy godmother get halfway through her *bibbedy-bobbedy-boos* and then wander off to watch the football? No! Magical assistants follow through with their promises, and you promised to assist me, so WHERE ARE YOU?!'

Not a peep. Nothing. Adam was on his own again. He was going to have to knuckle down and think up a bulletproof, unsinkable, sure-fire banger all by himself. But that was easier said than done, because there was a little something called PREPARING-FOR-A-HUGE-LIVE-SHOW-AT-THE-LONDON-ARENA eating away at every spare second of Adam's time. Rehearsals had begun, and even though it was cool to see it all coming together – dancers, music, fancy lights, indoor fireworks, a giant phone onstage to act like a big screen, surprise special guests (such big surprises that even Adam didn't know who most of them were yet!) – it left zero time for making videos. It was non-stop:

Meetings.

Rehearsals.

School.

Rehearsals.

Meetings.

Rehearsals.

School.

Rehearsals.

Rehearsals. *Rehearsals*. *REHEARSALS!*

He didn't have time for *anything*. On the last day of school – Adam worked. On the evening of the end-of-term disco – Adam worked. When they went on holiday to the caravan in County Cork – Adam worked the whole way through it. And on Saturday mornings he would try to scrape together enough time to create a video that people might want to watch.

He filmed Callum whizzing down the garden slide, straight into the paddling pool (which Adam had secretly filled with clear jelly). Ninety-one views.

He filmed his mum's reaction when she discovered that Adam had filled the entire oven, from bottom to top, with shaving foam. And the dishwasher. And the fridge. Sixty-four views.

He disguised himself as a hedge, plonked himself in the middle of the park and got Bruce to film him suddenly jumping to life and chasing other kids, who ran away, screaming for their lives. Seventy-six views.

These were rookie numbers.

What the actual fidgety fudge! OMG, what is happening with you, YouTube?!

Eventually Adam realised that 'small and fun' wasn't going to cut it. If he wanted to win back the internet he would have to go 'big and bold'. So he summoned Bruce and Callum to film a 'Big Surprise for My Little Brother' video, but when they arrived at their location, twenty metres from Adam's house, Callum didn't seem especially thrilled by the surprise Adam had lined up.

'Adam!' he yelled as Bruce filmed him. 'I didn't want to jump from a first-floor balcony into a

swimming pool! So what made you think I'd want to jump off *this* ...' he pointed up to the wobbly branch Adam was swaying on '... into *that?*' His finger tracked a path all the way down to the leaf-filled pool ten metres below.

Adam had scaled the mighty oak tree outside the O'Bannons' house in an attempt to show Callum just how simple it was.

'C'mon on up, Callum, it's pure easy!' He

attempted to make it seem like fun, but Callum looked like someone staring death in the face. 'And it's perfectly safe, too! I even checked that the height of the jump is safe for the depth of the pool, so that you don't shatter your head. Or your bottom. Or all your bones.'

'This is the worst surprise EVER!'

'Go on, ya little chicken, it's not even that high!' Bruce egged him on from behind the camera.

'I don't see *you* doing it!' Callum shot straight back.

'It could really help my channel!' Adam pleaded. 'Jumping from great heights, little kids in peril … people LOVE that stuff!'

'You said that *last time.*'

'And it's still *true!* It's fine, c'mon, climb up to me!'

'No!'

'Why?'

'Because …'

'Because why?'

'Because you'd never catch me up there, ever!'

'Because he's a little chicken,' Bruce jibed.

'Get lost, poo brea–'

Adam cut his insult short. 'Callum, look, all you need to do is grab this branch, then swing out like this ... Then once you swing you just, *aghhhh*, whoa, *WHOOOAAAA*!!!'

(Adam's demo did not go quite as planned. His foot slipped off the wobbly branch, causing the one he was holding to snap under his weight, sending him plummeting towards earth at breakneck speed. Down, *down*, *DOWN* he fell, followed by an almighty 'SPLOSH!')

'Wha-da BLUURG-CAAGGG!' Adam coughed, burped and snorted all in one go as he re-emerged from the cold leafy water. 'Tell me you g-g-g-got th-th-that.'

'Got it, man, all of it!' Bruce confirmed, before falling apart laughing. Even Callum shook his head in disbelief. Funniest. Video. Ever.

And the next day, when Adam checked his subs, his heart almost burst out of his mouth.

26

The Big Subs Boost
(Take Two)

It was the first day of August. Officially halfway through the summer holidays.

The numbers on Adam's clock read 0:71 – Seventy-one days until his time was up. Only *seventy* days until his live show.

And the views for Adam's latest video – 'I Fell Out of a Tree!' – were at a grand total of …

0

(Well, 132, which was practically the same as zero!)

Adam's subs had grown by a grand total of zero.

Adam's panic was at a grand total of ONE THOUSAND PER CENT.

Something had gone seriously wrong, but Adam had no idea *what*.

'I don't get it,' he complained to his empty room as he watched the perfectly good video play out on his channel. 'There's nothing the matter with this video! There's no reason people shouldn't be watching it in their thousands! There is no reason my subs should ...'

Adam's mouth fell open in horror as, just one minute into his video, a YouTube ad popped up, and he knew, in an instant, exactly why nobody had watched it.

'*You will NOT believe this cliff-jumping cat! WATCH NOW! WATCH NOW! WATCH NOW!*'

The advert was so short that you couldn't even skip it. And the three-second snippet of a cat sprinting towards the edge of a gigantic cliff was so intriguing you couldn't *not* click through to watch it. Even Adam clicked the link!

'I never stood a chance against this!' he whispered to himself as he watched the montage of Mr Floof make one death-defying jump after another into the crystal-clear waters of the Mediterranean. 'No one in their right mind would stick around to watch *me* tree-jumping when they could be watching this *cat* doing *cliffs*! No *wonder* I have no views!'

And it wasn't just *that* video. Every single one of Adam's uploads had fallen victim to ad-bait – adverts designed to lure viewers away from the video they're watching to go and watch something that looks even bigger and better. In the middle of his 'Unbelievable Bike Stunt in the Park' video was an ad for some random lady's old video called 'Five-Year-Old's Death-Defying Bike Stunt on a Skyscraper'. His giant teddy bear prank video had been hit with an ad for some college kid's prank – 'I Evacuated an Entire Cinema when I Dressed as a Zombie'! His skydiving video was now competing with '94-year-old Woman Skydiving on a Skateboard'! And his jet-ski water-fight was up against 'Giant Shark Interrupts Jet-Ski Paintball War'!

'Every single person coming to watch my videos is being poached!' Adam whimpered. '*Every single one!* Who would do this?! A rival YouTuber?'

It was completely possible, but for some reason it didn't feel like that was the answer. The Trojan Idiot knew exactly how to hurt Adam, almost *personally,* as if they knew him. But Adam still couldn't think of a single person who would resort to anything like this.

Whoever it was, Adam knew it was the exact same person who had sabotaged his WebCon speech. Who had wiped the footage from his phone and deleted the videos from his channel. This was no coincidence. Someone had spent hundreds of hours and thousands of pounds finding these videos and advertising them on his channel purely to make him fail.

'Somebody, somewhere wants to stop me reaching one million!' Adam gasped in realisation. 'That's why the Trojan Idiot has been attacking me!'

And the Trojan Idiot was succeeding. Adam's channel was suffocating. Dying. And there wasn't a single thing he could do to stop it. He looked down at his desk, to the framed photo of Dad.

'I wish I could just talk to you, tell you all my problems ...'

Dad wouldn't have any idea how to fix it – YouTube was never his thing – but he would have known exactly how to make Adam feel better, just like back when Adam had the starring role in the school play five years ago and the pressure was becoming too much for him.

'Pressure?' his dad had said. 'Pressure can *crush* you, like an egg in a vice. But, if you know how to handle it, pressure can shape you into something even stronger, like a piece of coal being compressed to become a diamond.'

'Yeah, but how is the school play going to turn me into a diamond? How can hundreds of people staring at me when I forget my lines be a *good* thing?'

His dad's response was to go to the kitchen cupboard, open up the tub where they kept all the birthday candles and matches and stuff, pull out two balloons, and hold them in the air, in front of Adam.

'What is pressure?' he asked little Adam.

'Horrible, that's what it is!'

'It's an enormous amount of concentrated

236

energy, *that's* what it is.'

He blew a huge lungful of air into the balloon.

'Now, when you're up onstage you can let that pressure build ...'

He blew again.

'And build ...'

He blew again, until the balloon was almost as big as it could go.

'And build ...'

Adam put his finger in his ears as Dad blew one more time.

'Until ...'

BANG! The balloon popped, and Adam jumped.

'Or ...' his dad continued, blowing into the second balloon. 'You can take control of that pressure.'

Blow ...

'You can *harness* its energy.'

Blow ...

'You can make it your own power source!'

Blow ...

'And you can use that energy to have fun! To put

BRA-A-A-A-A-A-A-A-A-A-A-A-P!

on a show! To help *everyone else* have fun! Like a world class cheerer-upper!'

And with that, Dad let go of the balloon and Adam erupted in laughter as it flew around the room like a bright red, farting tornado of fun!

Back at his desk Adam found himself laughing at the memory.

'Thanks, Dad.' He chuckled at the photo. 'That's exactly what I'll do. I'll use the pressure as my fuel. And this is so much pressure it's going to make *atomic* fuel! I'm not going to give up and burst like a balloon. I'm going to rocket myself forwards. I'm going to fight back with everything I've got. I'm going to pull out all the stops. I'm going to make the biggest video of my life. Something so big that no ad can ever compete. Do your worst, Trojan Idiot, because I am a warrior you will not

238

stop! This is war and I am ready for battle!'

'Adam!' his mum called from downstairs. 'Alphabetti Spaghetti!'

'I *will* be ready for battle –' he corrected himself – 'just as soon as I've had my Alphabetti Spaghetti.'

'My dad still talks about your dad all the time,' Bruce admitted when the two of them were walking back from the shops the next day, both munching from giant cups of Pick-n-Mix. 'He says that, back when they used to work together, your dad was the smartest person he'd ever met. And from what you just told me, all that stuff about using pressure as energy, I reckon he's right – your dad was an absolute genius!'

Adam wasn't sure he could ever like anyone as much as he liked Bruce right then.

'Your dad hit the nail on the head!' Bruce continued. 'That's exactly what *I* do when I'm feeling the pressure – I turn it into energy too! You know what I do?'

'What?' asked Adam, chuckling with anticipation.

'I do something that has given me the perfect idea for your next video.'

'What?!' Adam demanded, pretending to strangle the answer out of Bruce.

They were outside Adam's house now. Bruce stopped walking. He turned to Adam. His eyes lit up with electric enthusiasm. And then a whisper escaped his lips –

'I *smash ... things ... up!*'

Adam took a worried step back.

'Huh?'

'I destroy things! I release the pressure!'

'So ... your idea for my video is to ... *break things*?'

'Yes,' Bruce confirmed with a nod.

'Thinks like ... windows? Plates? Old computers?'

'Nuh-uh,' said Bruce with a shake of his head. 'I'm thinking bigger than that.'

'How big?'

'*MUCH* bigger.'

'Can you be a *bit* more specific?'

And that's where Bruce explained his whole idea for Adam's new video. And *that* was when Adam wondered if he may just have his hands on the BIGGEST BANGER the world would ever see.

The next two weeks were all about a new video, the whole video and nothing but the video. Adam skipped rehearsals, he ignored calls from Chris, 'accidentally forgot' about Studio Cre8 Zoom meetings, and instead focused all his attention on planning, prepping and paying out for his gimantuan new video. The scale of his idea was immense. 'Big and Bold' was nowhere near enough. No words in the English language were near enough. It was set to be 'Gimantuan and Blaurghh!'

And it meant a lot of hard work: he had to get written permissions from numerous people; he hired top tech guys to help with special effects; he even brought in professional camera operators to make sure he filmed the whole thing in all its magnificent glory, and all the while Bruce was right there, reassuring, back-patting, helping to arrange the whole thing.

When filming day finally came, Adam found he was so nervous he could barely eat a thing. There was so much to get right, so much that could go wrong. First of all he'd had to talk the rugby club into throwing a party so that he could be sure that almost everyone on his street would be out for the evening, and then, once they were gone, it was all systems go, all hands on deck, all now, now, NOW!

The projector team swooped in, the pyrotechnic experts set their equipment up, the camera oper-ators got into their hiding places, and the people from Car Hire for the Big Screen brought in their special vehicles. When Adam used up all of his energy, Bruce was right there, ready to take the controls, running the show like he'd been doing it his whole life. 'You! You need to be over there! Where's the smoke? Which idiot is in charge of the smoke? We need more! Come on! This is serious! It's not a children's party! Adam, look at this, it's

242

going to be SO cool. HEY! What are you DOING? Get into position! We've got TWO MINUTES! What is wrong with you people?! Let's go, *go, GO!*'

Then, once everything was in place and ready, they all waited, in perfect silence, until Adam's walkie-talkie crackled to life and Bruce's voice announced – 'They're coming! Get ready! They're coming! Right *now*.'

Adam's heart somersaulted with adrenalin as entire teams of people leaped into action and furious chaos exploded throughout the street.

Just three minutes later, one by one, his neighbours returned home to see flames dancing up the sides of their houses, huge holes blown through the walls, smoke filling the entire street, fire engines lined up with their lights flashing, and there, in the centre of it all, was Adam, his top half poking out of an army tank, one hand clutching his camera, the other hand planted across his forehead as he looked out among his ashen-faced, horror-stricken neighbours and proclaimed, over and over again – 'I'm so, so, so sorry! It was an accident! It was for a video! It ... it went so wrong! It wasn't supposed to happen like this! I'm so, so, so sorry! I'll pay for it all, I promise!'

Almost an entire minute passed before any of his neighbours recovered their wits enough to form the words to ask, 'What on earth *happened* here?!' And Adam could take it no longer. He howled with laughter as he called out, 'OK! Guys! Can we cut it?'

The smoke machines shut off and the air began to clear; the projectors that had been playing images of fire and destruction powered down and the walls of the houses transformed back their non-blown-up states of normalcy; the hired fire trucks drove off and the street was left looking almost completely back to normal, all except for Adam, giggling away in his tank, and a team of 'fire fighters' who turned around and revealed themselves as family members from the neighbourhood, who had all been in on the prank from the beginning. Bruce planted a massive bear hug on Adam. Their plan had come to life, and they'd executed it with military precision. It was sure to be the *best content* ever!

Adam spent the whole evening editing, trembling with excitement the entire time, and at 2 a.m. he finally clicked 'Upload' and allowed himself to collapse on to his bed, where he slept straight through until 10 a.m. And when he woke up and checked his YouTube page he was greeted by a sight that almost caused his brain to explode out of his ears.

27

The Big Subs Boost:
The Battle Is Over

It was officially the first day of September.

The numbers on Adam's clock read 0:40 – forty days until his time was up. *Thirty-nine* days until his live show.

And the views for Adam's latest video – 'I Pretended to Demolish My Entire Street!' – were at a grand total of …

0
(OK, so there was a 9 before that
zero, but 90 was still the lowest
number of views Adam had
ever had!)

Adam's subs had grown by a grand total of zero.

His panic was at a grand total of ONE MILLION PER CENT!

'There you go, Popularis,' Adam growled from his hot, sticky bed, which he just couldn't be bothered to get out of. 'I reached one million. Is that what your stupid riddle meant? Reach one million or lose all that you hold dear, that's what you said, isn't it? Well, look at me, I finally did it. I've reached one million on the panic scale. I've reached one million on the "I give up-o-meter". And the cost of all the stuff for that video – I've practically reached one million in *bills*! And you *lied*, because look – I *have* lost all that I hold dear! My channel is *dead*! It's gone! Nobody is watching it! I've lost it and I can't bring it back. So thanks for nothing, Popularis.'

Adam's angry rant was interrupted by an equally angry banging on the front door. Adam switched off his fan to better hear who it was. He heard the front door open, then his mum's tired voice –

'Morning, Jane. Everything OK?'

'Of course everything's not OK, Alice,' he heard Jane from over the road snap. 'I've got takeaway coffee cups all over my lawn and tyre tracks through my flower beds and *scorch marks* up the side of my house! It looks like the carnival has passed through here! And who's going to sort it all out? Adam's more than happy to put the hard work in when he's *preparing* his silly videos, but as soon as he's finished who's left to clear up the mess?'

'Jane, I ... I'm ...'

Adam listened as his mum stammered and struggled to explain and apologise and make promises and defend Adam all at the same time, and Adam couldn't bear it any longer.

'I'LL CLEAR IT UP LATER, OK? I PROMISED I WOULD AND I WILL!' he yelled towards his open window, still not bothering to get out of bed. 'THERE'S NO NEED TO BE SO RUDE ABOUT IT! YOU COULD JUST ASK POLITELY! JEEEZ! IT WAS JUST A *JOKE*! I'M SO SORRY IF NO ONE AROUND HERE HAS A SENSE OF HUMOUR!'

Jane began yelling something back up to him, but Adam turned his music on full blast before she even got three words in.

'AAAAARRGHHHHH!' he roared as he thumped his fists into his pillow, over and over again.

'I QUIT! I QUIT! I QUIT!'

And he wasn't joking. Adam had officially given up. He'd tried to win this. He'd given it *everything*. But it wasn't enough. It was over. No more. Slimeboy Adam was over. *Everything* was over. Goodbye cool Adam, hello School Adam.

He stopped caring about views and subs, he stopped caring about all the 'urgent' calls and messages and emails he was ignoring from Chris, he stopped caring about *everything*. And soon enough, the rest of the world became nothing but a blur.

He didn't notice that he'd stopped brushing his hair. He didn't notice the letters on the kitchen table from the credit card company, demanding his mum pay them back the money she'd borrowed to pay for months of train tickets, bus tickets and taxis to work. And as he walked with Callum, for his first ever day of secondary school, he didn't notice how Callum's hands were trembling with nerves. Nor did he notice Ethan, walking by himself just fifty metres behind, dodging the ice-cold water balloons being pelted at his head. Nor did he notice that the person doing the pelting was Bruce Kilter, or that the whole thing was being filmed as a 'Hilarious Prank' for Bruce's very own channel.

'See ya, Adam,' said Callum as he headed towards the school doors for the first time. 'Love you.'

But Adam didn't notice Callum's goodbye. He didn't see the look of longing as Callum hoped to hear 'Love you one million' in return, or perhaps a 'Love you one thousand', or even a *one hundred*. And he didn't notice that, as Callum passed a laughing, rowdy group of kids hanging by the school doors, his pace slowed, his feet began to shuffle and his lips began mouthing the words *'Head down. Don't react. They'll get bored soon and leave you alone.'*

Adam had his own problems to worry about, and they felt so much bigger than anyone else's.

From that day on, Adam decided to shut himself away in his room and busy himself making small and simple videos, just for himself, with no intention of ever uploading them, with no pressure of viewer numbers or subs or ad-bait. It would be just like it used to, back in the good old days. He filmed himself practising magic tricks, or messing around with dominoes, or trying to get a screwed-up ball of paper into his bin without even looking. And, very slowly, Adam began enjoying himself again.

'Hey, Adam,' said a voice from the half-open door of Adam's bedroom. Adam had been so engrossed in his task (trying to fit a tiny camera inside a tennis ball) that the voice at his door caused him to literally leap halfway across his room in shock.

'Ethan! Oh my *life*! You scared the *bejeepers* out of me!'

'Sorry!' Ethan laughed, but it wasn't his usual laugh. It was quiet and shy when it should have been rolling-on-the-floor hysterics at the sight of Adam's terror.

'I know we don't really hang out any more, but I was just wondering if we could talk about something?'

Adam tamped down the flash of guilt that Ethan's words gave him and tried to sound breezy.

'Yeah, of course, man! Any time! Come in! What do you want to talk about?'

'It's nothing really, just something that's been bothering me at school, and, well, I was wondering if you could help.'

'Ethan, of course!' Adam laughed to see his friend acting so nervous around him. 'Spit it out! What's up?'

'Well, it's kind of something you've already dealt with in the past,' Ethan began, perching himself on the edge of Adam's bed. 'Or ... someone ... and, well ...' Ethan paused, cocking his head as he eyed the graveyard of decapitated tennis balls all over Adam's bedroom floor. 'What are you *doing*?'

'I actually have *no* idea!' Adam laughed. 'I just thought it would look really cool if I could fit a GoPro in a tennis ball, then see what kind of videos I could get just chucking it around the garden, or smacking it way up into the air. Actually, I'm glad you came round because I could really use a second pair of hands to get it in there!'

And whatever it was that Ethan had come round to talk about got completely lost in an entire day of messing around in the garden, playing with balls, making stupid video after stupid video, laughing their heads off, just like old times, until they finally collapsed in the shade of the garden hedge and filled their bellies with ice cream and lemonade.

'You know what we should do now?' Ethan said with wide-eyed excitement. 'We should do one of those videos where you roll a ball and it knocks something down, and that thing knocks another thing, then another ball rolls down a plank of wood and knocks three other things down ...'

'A chain reaction video!' Adam gasped. 'We so should! Let's do it!'

And three hours later, after dozens of failed attempts, they finally had their masterpiece all set up and ready for action.

'Ethan ...' Adam whispered in awe as the two of them stood back to admire their epic creation. It ran all around Adam's bedroom, out of the window, down the side of the house and across the front garden. 'This ... is going to be ...'

'No! Oh no, no, no!' Ethan gasped, checking his phone for the first time since he'd arrived. 'I was supposed to be home, like, *four hours ago*! My mum's gonna *murder me*! I gotta go!'

Five seconds later Ethan was racing down the road on his bike, calling over his shoulder to Adam up in his bedroom window.

'I hope it works! Send me the link as soon as you've filmed it! Good luck!'

'You too!' Adam called back. 'I hope your mum doesn't murder you *too* much!'

So, back on his own once again, Adam continued their good work, and began filming the video before it got too dark to see anything.

'OK, I haven't tried this all in one go yet, but this is what I *hope* is going to happen,' he quietly told the camera as he nervously set up the first stage of the stunt. 'I'm going to push this toy car across my

desk, and it'll fall off the edge, into the cardboard tube. Down the tube, out the other end, on to the wooden-spoon see-saw. This end of the spoon should come down and switch the fan on. The other end, with the ping-pong ball on it, should go up, catapulting the ping-pong ball up and into the mini basketball hoop. When it drops out of the hoop, the fan should blow the ball on to this shelf, sending these dominoes falling.

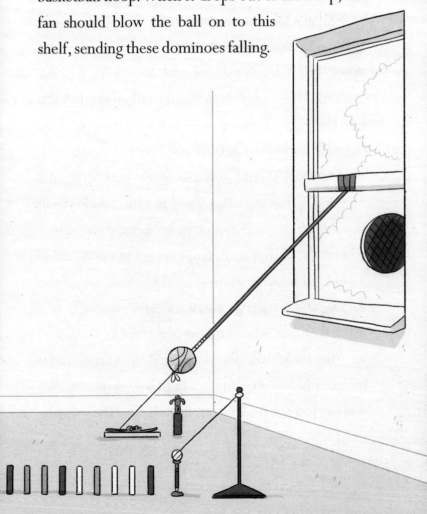

The final domino should topple the remote control, the remote control should knock over the DVD, the DVD should knock over this book, and the book should knock the tennis ball off the other end of the shelf and straight out of my bedroom window.'

Adam paused for breath, then, for the first time in a long while, he felt a genuine surge of excitement as he rushed over to the window and threw it open. 'But it doesn't stop there!' he chuckled to the camera. 'The tennis ball should fall straight down into the gutter of our porch, below, where there's a football waiting to get knocked by the tennis ball. The football should roll along the gutter, hit the bowling ball at the other end, and the bowling ball should roll down the other side of our garage roof, where – you can't see it from here, but my portable basketball hoop is waiting on the other side of the garage, don't worry, one of the other cameras will catch that shot when I do the actual trick – it should hit the basketball backboard, drop through the hoop, roll down Callum's old plastic slide – which you can just see peeking out from behind the garage –

hit these giant dominoes in the front garden, which are basically big chunks of wood that I painted black, and the last and tallest domino should hit the branch of that tree, which should knock down the marble I've balanced on the end of that twig, where – *fingers crossed, I hope, hope, HOPE* – it will land in that tiny wee egg cup that I decorated myself when I was a sweet and innocent six-year-old. And then … my mind-blowingly magnificent trick … will be COMPLETE! And I will probably run around celebrating like a total idiot because, I am not joking, this has taken me and my friend Ethan *so, so* long to prepare. Hours! Days! *Weeks!* No, well, actually just hours, but seriously, if this works, I will be … Oh my life, I don't even know. It'll be amazing! OK. Are you ready? Then here goes …'

He paused for a while, allowing the enjoyment of it all to rush through him, then he carried on, talking to no one, but imagining a million people were watching.

'Get ready for something spectacular!' He rolled the toy car across his desk and watched with bated breath as it sped towards the cardboard tube and then ... it missed the tube completely and plummeted straight into his wastepaper bin.

'NO! What a terrible beginning! Pretend it didn't happen!'

Adam quickly fished the car out of the bin, dropped it back on the desk and gave it another push with his finger. Perfect shot! It rolled straight into the cardboard tube, on to the wooden spoon and – yes! – the fan went on! The ping-pong ball went flying through the mini basketball hoop, Adam gasped with triumph as the fan blew the ball on to the shelf. It hit the first domino smack bang in the centre, the first domino hit the second, the second hit the third and down went the rest with a *klacka-tacka-tack*! Down went the remote control, then the DVD, then the book, then *POK!* went the tennis ball, straight out of the window! A rooftop camera caught the tennis ball as it *swooshed* through the open window, then smacked into the back of the football in the gutter, and the football went ... nowhere. It just sat there.

Adam's palms slammed into his forehead as a pained 'Noooooooo!' squeaked out of his throat. But wait! The football moved! It rocked forwards. The rock became a roll. Little by little it crept along the gutter, but it soon picked up speed, faster and faster until it was rumbling along at a pace and then – *BOINK!* – it bounced into the bowling ball, pushing it effortlessly off the edge of the gutter and down the sloping garage roof. The driveway cam caught the moment the bowling ball came careering down the roof and straight towards the backboard of the portable basketball hoop, and ... no! The basketball hoop wasn't there! It was on the ground, lying flat on its back! *How could that be?!* There was nothing to stop the bowling ball's trajectory! It flew off the garage roof and ... *it crashed straight through the neighbour's window*! A startled cat went shooting out of the neighbour's cat flap, across the front lawn and straight into the path of an oncoming car. The car swerved. The brakes screamed. Then it slammed to a halt as it crashed into ... *Adam's bright yellow tennis ball, which had bounced in front of it. Whooooosh!* went the tennis ball as it soared higher and higher, like a tiny spherical rocket hurtling towards outer space. Up, up, up it went!

Adam's heart was in his throat. He couldn't move. He couldn't *breathe*. How was his stunt going so wrong?! His eyes strained to follow the ball, which was now nothing but a tiny yellow speck. He wondered if it was ever going to come back down. And then it did, slowly, slowly, then faster, faster, then *WHAM*! It shuttled through the open window of a big yellow digger that was busy laying the foundations for a new house over the road. The driver gave a yelp, clutched his face, tumbled from the cab and landed in a pile of dirt as the digger rumbled along without him, like a mischievous child who'd given his teacher the slip. *Crunch!* went a telegraph pole as the digger ploughed into it. *Thwunk!* went the next telegraph pole as the first one fell into it. *Clonk!* went the third pole as that fell too. *Bam!* went the fourth. *Donk! – Boof! – Crack! – Klunk! –*

And as every telegraph pole on the other side of the street went down like a series of impossible dominoes, a taxi pulled up outside Adam's house, and his mum climbed out of it, her arms loaded with bulging grocery bags. 'Thank you so much, Trevor,' she called to the driver as she closed the door, completely oblivious to the chaos that was running away down the street. 'And remember to tell your wife about peppermint tea. My sister swears by it!'

At the other end of the street, the final telegraph pole fell, so far away that there was barely a sound, until – *THWANG!* – it crashed straight on to the roof of a Coffee to Go-Go! delivery van, knocking the giant plastic coffee cup from the top and sending it careering down the sloping road. Bouncing and spinning, tumbling and bounding, faster and faster went the oversized coffee cup as it hurtled down the hill. Panic punched Adam in the heart as he realised that the out-of-control ornament was on a direct collision course with –

'MUM!' Adam roared as his collection of cameras all burst into blinding brightness in their various positions around the garden –

FLASH!

A jolt of electricity kicked him in the brain.

FLASH!

A deafening screech tore at his ears.

FLAAAAAAASHHHHH!

'MUM! LOOK OUT!'

But Adam's warning was drowned out by Trevor the taxi driver's honk of his horn as he waved goodbye and drove off in the opposite direction to the five-foot coffee cup that was rocketing through the air towards Adam's mum. And then it landed – *CRACK!* – on the exact spot where Adam's mum was standing.

No amount of watching and rewatching the video helped make any sense of what had happened. *No* sense! One minute his mum was there in the middle of the road, the next minute the giant cup smashed down, and Mum was in the middle of their driveway, *four metres away*! Except it wasn't 'the next minute', it was *less than a second*! No one can move that far so

quickly! Itching with confusion, Adam played the video back in super-slo-mo, one frame at a time, like a series of still pictures, and then he saw how it had happened – Mum hadn't jumped, she hadn't been knocked over, she had *walked* it! In ten frames! That's not even half a second! It was as if she had been speeded up. As if someone had pressed fast forward on her life. And Adam knew exactly who that 'someone' was.

'Popularis?' Adam whispered, slumped below his bedroom window as he stared at the screen of his camera. 'You're back!'

And it wasn't just Popularis who was back – Adam had a feeling, deep down inside him, that Slimeboy Adam was also back. Dizzy with excitement, Adam raced to his computer and was just about to upload the video when a horrible thought dawned on him.

I have just wrecked the entire street … for REAL! But no one knows it was me. No one saw a thing! And now I have this video — the one thing that could save my channel, but … If I upload it, then everyone will know exactly who did it!

Adam paused. His cursor hovered over the upload button. His brain whirred at a million miles per hour.

'I'd get so many more visits from angry neighbours,' Adam warned himself with a grimace of dread. 'And so many repairs to pay for … And police to explain to! And…'

Click.

The video went live. Out across the internet, for everyone to see.

'This *really* better be worth it.'

And the next morning, as he plucked up the courage to open up his YouTube app and check his stats, his entire body almost turned itself inside out and burst from his nostrils at what he saw …

28

It's All Over

It was the first day of October.

The numbers on Adam's clock read 0:11 — eleven days until his time was up. *Ten* days until his live show.

And the views for Adam's latest video — 'I ACTUALLY Demolished My Entire Street!' — were at a grand total of ...

1.3 MILLION!

Adam's subs had grown to *889k*!

Adam's panic was at a grand total of 'EAT *THAT*, TROJAN IDIOT! YES! I BEAT YOU! I TOTALLY BEAT YOU!' (Also known as 'zero'.)

School Adam was dead! Cool Adam was back! Slimeboy Adam reigned supreme!

The Trojan Idiot had attempted to attack the upload with another round of ad-bait, but Adam's natural talent at creating complete and absolute chaos proved too powerful for it. The ad-bait had failed. Adam's channel burst back to life. One by one, *all* the Trojan Idiot's ad-baits began to lose their power, toppling like dominoes. Adam's views went through the roof! His subs went soaring! Hashtag Slimeboy was trending once more, along with the words 'London Arena' and 'live show' and 'tickets on sale!'

OK, so, yes, Adam did have to deal with a barrage of complaints from furious neighbours. And yes, he did have to explain himself to the police (who, luckily, saw the funny side and agreed that it really was an honest accident), and he did have to spend immense amounts of money on helping to repair the street, but it was worth it. His video was a hit! His channel was alive! He became better friends with his neighbours than ever before. He managed to talk the police into letting him film a 'Real Life

Prison Break' video down at the station. And, by some miracle, after coughing up for all the repairs, he still had *just* enough money to make the final payment for Mum's new car next week. Adam couldn't remember the last time he'd felt this good.

But it wasn't all plain sailing. He still had some very awkward explaining to do. Firstly to Chris and the people at the London Arena, telling them the truth — 'I'm so sorry I didn't get back to you, I was so busy sorting out my latest video. So, what did you want to talk about? It sounded kind of urgent!'

'Nothing to worry about!' came their various replies. 'There was a slight problem, but it seems to have sorted itself out.' And by that, Adam knew they meant — 'We were worried no one wanted to come and see your show, but that's all changed now!'

That was the easy part. It was the 'explaining to Mum' bit that wasn't so simple.

'Adam, we really need to talk,' she told him, cornering him in his bedroom one evening.

'I know what you're going to say — I need to be more careful, I need to dial it back, not be so reckless, be more conscientious when making my videos — and

I totally agree and I promise I totally will from now on.'

He reeled it off so quickly, so seamlessly, so perfectly, making sure to face Mum square-on, with the best puppy-dog eyes of all time, and with his praying hands pleading so mercifully that it *almost* seemed as though he had *rehearsed* it. A lot. And Mum seemed to think so too.

'Yes, Adam, that was very impressive, but listen to me ... I know you've done a great job at calming down the neighbours, but some of them are still *very* angry, and I'm spending all of my spare time trying to patch things up with them, as well as spending all of my spare money trying to *fix* things up for them, and ...'

'I'll make it up to you, I promise!'

If only I could tell her about the car! Adam silently pleaded with himself. *She'd be so happy! But it's going to make such a great video and I can't ruin it!*

'I'm not finished, Adam. Please don't interrupt,' his mum continued, growing sterner by the second. 'All I ask is that you try to be a bit more considerate in your actions! You don't seem to understand how much hard work it is looking after you two on my own. The shopping, the cooking, the bills, the spending all of my life at work to pay for everything, and all without a car. I just don't have the energy for so much extra chaos, Adam. I don't have the *time*. I ...'

'Mum, I *am* considerate!' Adam insisted. 'I ...'

'Well, you have a funny way of showing it! Instead of *helping* me you just make my life so much *harder*! These videos ... yes, I'm happy that you've found so much success, but ...'

'Mum, these videos ... I do them for *you*!'

'For *me*?!' His mum gave an incredulous laugh. 'Adam, you almost *killed me*!'

'No! I didn't! I had it all under control!'

'Under control? So you mean you *planned* that? You almost had me crushed to death as part of a *stunt*?'

'No! I don't mean that! I mean ...'

Adam gave up trying to explain. Telling her that he had his magical internet algorithm looking out for her wasn't going to make things better. So he stopped there.

'Sorry, Mum,' he said, head bowed. 'You're right. But I *will* make it up to you. As soon as my show is over I'll make it all better, I *promise*.'

'I hope so, Adam,' she said as she left the room. 'I really do.'

Adam's heart gave a little squeeze. Getting that car for Mum now seemed more important than ever. But with the show just around the corner Adam knew it wasn't going to be long. He was going to make the biggest success of it. He had to. And with the Chain Reaction banger under his belt, and with Popularis back in his corner he knew it was possible. He was unstoppable, he convinced himself. *Invincible.* Just a few more days and Adam would be gliding into London, for a week that would prove to be even bigger than *GIMANTUAN* – it was going to be the most important few days of his life.

29

The Wait Is Over

BOOOOOOOOOOOOOOOOOOM!
It was a sound that should have zipped through Adam's veins like electric joy.

KARRUMM-RAKKA-BOOOOOM!

It was a sound that ought to have made him want to leap and cheer and punch the air with excitement.

KA-BOOM-CHAKKA-CHA-CHA-KARRA-BOOOM!

But from deep in the belly of the London Arena, the thunderous rumble of thousands of fans arriving was not a sound Adam was enjoying. It sounded like pure terror. It sounded like war drums. It sounded like a plague of zombies waiting to tear him to pieces. And instead of zipping through his veins like electric joy, it was creeping through his veins like poisonous treacle.

The room backstage was cold and quiet and completely empty except for Adam, Chris, a time-lapse camera he'd set up in the corner of the room to capture all the pre-show 'fun', and a line of tables piled high with 68.4 billion kajillion T-shirts, baseball caps and posters that Adam was trying to autograph before the show began.

'Is Bruce here yet?' He tried his best to sound casual and not terrified, but his trembling hands gave him away. (His autograph looked like it had been written by a blindfolded squirrel trying to write with its toes!)

'How many people are out there? It sounds like *quite a few*. And what about my final mystery guest? Do we even know who it is yet? Wow, it's cold in here, right? Do you know where Mum and Callum have gone?'

'First things first,' said Chris, exuding calmness and reassurance with every syllable, 'let's lay off the caffeine for a while, eh? You've just signed the desk for the sixteenth time in a row. Secondly,' Chris continued, moving Adam's energy drink aside as he perched on the edge of the desk, 'no, Bruce isn't here yet, but that's no problem, he's only got a walk-on part. One of the dancers can fill in if he doesn't show. And thirdly, yes, we do know who your mystery guest is.'

Actually, Chris had known who Adam's mystery guest was for *months*, he just hadn't told Adam because he didn't want him freaking out any more than he already was.

Adam stared up at him, his marker pen pressing down on a T-shirt so hard that a big black stain was soaking through the entire stack.

'Well?!' Adam urged. '*Who is it?!?!*'

'Oh, you know, nobody special,' Chris teased as he calmly removed the pen from Adam's hand.

'Chris! *Who?!*'

'Ahhh, well … just some small-time YouTuber you've probably never heard of.'

'*Chris!*'

'All right! All right! It's some guy called … oh, what was his name? Mighty Eddie? Ed-might? Edward Mighty Hands?'

Adam jumped to his feet with such speed that his chair flew back and his thighs tipped the desk over, with Chris on top.

'No way!' Adam gasped. 'NO! WAY! *ED ALMIGHTY?!* ARE YOU KIDDING ME?!'

'Thought you might be a little bit pleased,' Chris chuckled as he clambered out from beneath a mountain of T-shirts.

Adam had to sit on the floor and hold his head between his legs while he tried to stop hyperventilating. 'Ed Almighty ... in *my* show ... *Ed Almighty!*' he kept muttering to himself over and over again until, eventually, he calmed down enough to ask, 'What about the turnout? You never told me how many people are here. How many tickets did we sell in the end?'

'Adam,' said Chris with eyes as wide as saucers and a grin to match. 'We're *sold out*!'

It was official – Adam was now the most freaked-out person in the entire history of the human race. And beyond.

'IT'S SOLD OUT?! ED ALMIGHTY?! *AND* IT'S SOLD OUT? ARE YOU *SERIOUS*? OH MY LIFE!

SOLD OUT! *AND* ED ALMIGHTY! *THE* ED ALMIGHTY? IN *MY* SHOW? MY *SOLD-OUT* SHOW! WITH ED ALMIGHTY!!!'

Adam was practically ready to pass out when – *CLANG!* The door burst open and in spilt a flood of friends, family and guests, all laughing, cheering and jostling.

'Here we go, buddy! Yeay!' wailed Joanne as she ran across the room and leaped on to Adam's back.

'My wee mucker has made it ... woo hoo!' shouted Lee, in what Adam could only assume was an attempt at an Irish accent.

More and more guests and friends arrived by the minute until the entire backstage area was buzzing with noise and chaos. To the grown-ups it looked like a classroom full of out-of-control kids who'd had too much sugar. To everyone else, it looked like the party that dreams were made of, filled to the brim with social media royalty. Adam had hoped that all the people and the noise would drown out his sickening nerves, but it had the opposite effect – his sickening nerves just got louder. Not even Lee and Joanne were distraction enough, and

Adam found himself gravitating towards the only two people he really wanted to be with.

'Nerves getting to you?' Mum guessed, not even needing to wait for an answer.

'Look, I know things have been a bit, well, tough lately.' She smiled and they all knew what she meant.

'I think we've all been through a lot. Me, you, Callum, everyone on our street has, ha ha, but that's behind you now. This is your time to shine, you made this happen.' She paused. 'I think we're all a little nervous right now.' She pulled Adam into a hug, and Callum did his bit too, by touching Adam's elbow with his little finger. Adam's heart pounded with nerves, excitement and happiness, he knew that the car reveal would make everything better, complete, worthwhile and Mum would finally see why he pushed so hard and why he obsessed so much, this was it, the journey was almost over.

'I do have a few little butterflies zooming around inside ma belly!'

'You *should* be nervous!' Mum laughed. 'Twenty thousand people have all come to see *you*! But, Adam, listen to me,' she held him at arm's length and looked him in the eyes, 'they have come to see the *real you*, Adam, the real you who gets nervous, who messes up, who makes a fool of himself ... I think they'd be disappointed if they *didn't* see that. So embrace your fear, let your nerves be your friends and they'll see you right.'

It was weird because it *actually worked* – being told it was OK to feel nervous actually stopped him from feeling so nervous. And before long, Adam found he was enjoying himself backstage. Enjoying himself so much that he almost forgot what he was there for. He almost forgot that it was *his* show they were all there to see. Enjoying himself so much that he completely lost track of time, until—

'Adam!' Chris called. 'What are you still doing here? They've been calling for you! You're onstage in *three minutes*!'

Chaos! Confusion! Rushing! Running! Angry whispers! Urgent yelling! Lights! Cables! Hair! Make-up! Jacket!

'You OK, buddy?' asked the intensely muscular sound technician attaching Adam's radio mic with superhuman speed. 'Nerves getting to you?'

'Erm … well … I …'

'Looks like you're up!'

'What?!'

Like a crack of thunder, a voice boomed throughout the arena –

'LADIES AND GENTLEMEN! BOYS AND GIRLS! THE WAIT IS OVER …'

Adam felt a nine thousand butterflies burst to life in his belly.

30

The Big, Huge, Gimantuan Show

'THE TIME IS NOW! THE MOMENT HAS COME! PLEASE PUT YOUR HANDS TOGETHER AND WELCOME YOUR FAVOURITE YOUTUBE SENSATION – SLIMEBOYYYY ADAAAAAAAAAM!'

Thunderous applause. Deafening cheers. Trembling kneecaps. Adam drew a sharp breath, clapped his hands together, stepped out on to the stage and … jumped straight into an oversized coffee cup and rolled himself into a series of prop telegraph poles, knocking them down like skittles. He popped out of the cup right in the centre of the stage, landing perfectly on his mark. He stood up, paused in the madness, basked in the adoration, then made his intro:

'Hello everyone, welcome to the show, I'm Adam, Slimeboy Adam, and tonight I'm gonna take you on a fun-filled, prank-challenge-fest like you've never seen before!' The crowd went nuts.

'ARE YOU READYYYYYYYY?' His voice was barely audible through the noise.

'WOOOOAAAAARRRRRRRR!' It felt like a thunderstorm; ten thousand voices came back at him like a herd of wild horses.

'I said … ARE YOU READYYYYYYY?!'

The roof almost came off the London Arena, the crowd took it to the next level.

'WOOOOAAAAARRRRRRRRRSSSSHHHHHHH!'

'Let's bring on the dancers!' The music kicked in, sending bass-drum shock waves through Adam's chest. Freestylers emerged in perfect unison from each side of the stage, slowly moving inwards, circling Adam with each beat, Adams heart lifted, this was it, for tonight, he was KING!

Wave after wave of laughter went crashing over him, filling him with strength, buoying him with reassurance, inflating him with gratitude, and from that moment on, Adam's nerves were a mere speck on the distant horizon. He was loving every second of it – the energy, the spectacle, the sheer volume and size of it all. The rehearsals had paid off – the dancers, the music, the perfectly timed appearances of Callum on the screen of that giant phone in the centre of the stage, the laughter, the applause, the adrenalin – it was like magic! Adam had never felt so alert, so energised, so *alive*.

The first of the four segments went by like a precision-made piece of machinery – the first guests came and went; the audience laughed and gasped at all the right moments.

The second segment was so slick, so streamlined it left the first segment eating its dust.

The second guests came and went. All the while the pace was quickening, the momentum growing, the laughter increasing, the enjoyment snowballing.

A routine with Adam back in the teddy bear costume, chasing the dancers off the stage with a bottle of shampoo in one hand and a bottle of glue in the other had people literally rolling in the aisles.

It was beginning to feel like a sport, the perfect game, one goal after another – bam! Bam! BAM!

They were over halfway through.

Ed Almighty's appearance was coming up.

The gigantic slime-fest was on its way.

The big finale was inching closer.

The atmosphere was buzzing.

The air was electric.

Every two seconds his attention would be caught by someone in the crowd with a wave, or a sign. He'd got used to that, but just then, his gaze alighted on a person standing in the shadow of the wings. It was a boy, Adam thought, from the silhouette, about the same age as him.

'Huh?' This wasn't rehearsed, *do we have a rogue fan?*

Adam's eyes darted to Chris. He gestured to the shadowy figure.

And all of a sudden the stage was …

Black.

Complete and utter darkness swamped the entire arena.

No lights.

No sound.

And then came the alarms.

Followed by the screams.

The harsh, cold emergency lighting.

The panic.

The confusion.

And …

Slimeboy Adam had left the building.

31

Absolute Zero

Adam was propelled through the overcrowded, panic-filled exit tunnel. Bright lights. Shoving. Shouting. Stumbling. Adam was spat out into the cold, still darkness of the night, repeatedly muttering a question that was lost among the dozens of other voices all asking the same thing – *What's happening?!*

Chris appeared by Adam's side, ending a call with the arena security team as he announced to Adam –

'It's not good.'

Callum and Mum rushed over.

'What's going on?!'

'No one really knows,' Chris told the three of

them. 'The power went out. The fire alarm was tripped … no fire though. It was a hoax. Triggered manually. Plus a few people have reported seeing someone acting suspiciously, lurking around back-stage, so … I'm really sorry, Ad. They're cancelling the rest of the show. It's a security risk.'

'*Cancelling?* But we're barely halfway through!'

'I know,' Chris sighed, looking just as crushed as Adam.

'We're *sold out*!'

'I know,' Chris sighed again, putting a hand on Adam's shoulder.

'And … and … and … *Ed Almighty!*' Adam continued.

And then as if by some weird and horribly timed coincidence the YouTube power house turned the corner, being ushered along by his team. Adam held out an apologetic hand.

'Ed … I don't even know …' Adam's lip quivered, his voice shook, he felt tears well up in his eyes.

'Look, man, don't worry about it.' Adam knew Ed was just being nice. He could obviously see that

Adam was broken. 'You wanna see some of the crazy weird malfunctions I've had! Believe me, this is fine, you'll bounce back!'

He gave Adam a brief hug before being pushed onwards. Adam held back a thousand tears.

Then, from the end of the corridor, Ed looked back.

'Adam, mate, you're *ONE HECK* of an entertainer, don't forget that!'

That was all it took, the waterworks took over. Adam was a mess.

'Let's head back to the hotel, yeah? We'll grab Lee and Joanne too, and we'll try to see the night out in good spirits?' suggested Chris, doing his best to sound upbeat.

'I just want to go home, Chris,' Adam groaned, sitting himself down on the cold pavement, with his head in his hands. 'How is this actually happening?'

Head down. Brain off. Reality will get bored soon and leave me alone.

'C'mon, Adam, let's go.' Mum offered a comforting hand on his shoulder. 'You were brilliant tonight, just brilliant.' She too was holding back some tears.

Adam felt multiple vibrations in his pocket, he stood up and pulled out his phone and, as he did, four messages pinged on to his screen –

You have 1 missed call
You have 2 missed calls
You have 3 missed calls ...
You have 1 new voicemail

Adam didn't recognise the number. A part of him hoped that maybe it was the arena stage manager calling to say, 'Adam! We're ready for you back onstage!'

No such luck.

'Good evening, Mr Beales, it's Elaine from Mercedes here.' Adam moved off to the side for some privacy. 'I'm just calling about your purchase plan, and wanted to let you know as soon as I could that I'm afraid we won't be able to carry out the delivery of your eVito Tourer Pro L3 tomorrow, as

I'm afraid your funds haven't cleared. If you could call me back as soon as is convenient, we can final-ise your payment and get your delivery back on track. My number is ...'

Mum's car was not coming.

'Why?!' Adam roared at his phone. 'Why *me*?!'

Not wanting to see another one of his plans ruined, Adam instantly opened his banking app to try to send the payment to the dealership from there. He couldn't let Mum down again. Not after all this. But when the app opened, Adam froze in utter horror.

'What the ... ?'

'What's up now, Adam?' asked Callum.

Adam slowly looked up at him, with a face as grey as ash, and quietly explained –

'I've been robbed.'

There, on his screen, was the total amount of savings in his account ...

0.00

32

Unmasking the
Trojan Idiot

It was morning. Not just any morning – Adam's favourite kind:

- Sunny
- Warm
- Lazy
- And best of all ...

'WE WERE SOLD OUT!' Adam wailed as he slammed his head into his pillow over and over again, as if somehow his bedding was to blame for the entire London Arena fiasco.

Sorry. There was no 'best of all'. It was a trick. It

wasn't Adam's 'favourite kind' of *anything*. The entire morning pretty much sucked beyond belief.

'We were *sold out!*' he groaned into his pillow. 'Ed Almighty! And we were *sold out!*'

Today was the day. Exactly one year on from the first time he'd met Popularis. The precise day that Adam was supposed to 'Reach one million, or lose all you hold dear.' But instead of skyrocketing past his one million deadline, like he'd predicted, his subs had fallen from 997k to 992k.

Mum tried over and over again to persuade him to get out of bed, to come downstairs, to eat something, but it turns out that all Adam was capable of doing was punching his pillow, pulling his blanket over his head and groaning very, very loudly.

There was another knock at his door, followed by the sound of footsteps gingerly creeping in.

'Go away, Mum!' Adam growled with his face still submerged in his pillow.

'Hey, Adam, it's me.'

'Go away, Ethan. I'm not in the mood.'

'I know,' said Ethan. 'That's why I'm here.'

'*That's why you're here?*' Adam lifted his face from

his pillow. 'What, you've had enough of seeing me succeed in life, so you thought you'd come and gloat at me while I'm down?!'

'No,' Ethan said firmly. 'Adam, I just …'

'Just *what*, Ethan?' Adam glowered, now sitting up in his bed. 'You just want to rub it in, how big I failed? You just want to remind me how much I messed up? Well, guess what, Ethan? I ALREADY KNOW ALL OF THAT! *HAPPY?!*'

'What is *up* with you, Adam?' Ethan shot back. 'Why would any of that make me happy?'

'Oh, I don't know! Let me see! Perhaps because you're jealous? Because I made something of my life? Because I got a new friend?'

'Forget it, Adam. See you later.' Ethan quickly turned to leave, but Adam wasn't done.

'Bit of a coincidence though, isn't it? How someone knew the *exact* video to embarrass me the most at WebCon, and *you're* the only person outside this family who knew that video existed! How you were the first one to spot those videos being deleted from my account, and you're the only other person who knows my YouTube password! In fact, we've been friends so long you probably know *all* my pass-words, don't you, Ethan? You probably even know the password for my bank!'

'What are you even talking about?!'

'Oh, and what a coincidence – we spent hours setting up that chain reaction vid, everything was in its right place, and then you run off home and *whoops* somehow the basketball hoop's mysteriously fallen over! How could you possibly think I wouldn't suspect you straight away? You are the worst friend I've ever had, Ethan! You drove the whole street

against me, you destroyed public property, you nearly killed my mum, for God's sake! But I guess that was the plan all along – to hurt me as much as you can. Well, guess what? It didn't work! It backfired! Your sabotage made that video one of my biggest bangers of all time!' Adam delivered verbal devastation with a fierce scowl.

'Don't even get me started about the London show! You couldn't even be bothered to turn up, the biggest night of my life. At least Bruce had the decency to apologise for missing it!' His eyes

pierced right through Ethan's soul.

'Or, no … Hold on, maybe you *were* there, huh? Maybe that was you I saw, standing in the shadows just before the power went out and the fire alarm went off? Another part of your devious scheme, eh? Wreck the show. Why not, you've wrecked everything else? WHO ARE YOU?'

'Adam,' growled Ethan with a furious glare in his eye. 'You didn't see me at the show because I wasn't there. And the reason I wasn't there was because you *didn't invite me*! Why would I apologise for not turning up to a show I wasn't invited to? You're the one who should be apologising, Adam! You're the one who's a bad friend!' Ethan stormed out of the room, shot down the stairs and marched straight out of the front door.

'SO THAT'S WHY YOU DID IT?!' Adam yelled out of his window, after him. 'THAT'S WHY YOU RUINED MY LIFE? BECAUSE I'M NOT A GOOD FRIEND? BECAUSE I GOT ANOTHER FRIEND WHO WASN'T YOU? AND ALL THIS TIME I KEPT SUSPECTING *BRUCE*! YOU'RE NOTHING BUT A COWARD, ETHAN, AND YOU'RE

GONNA PAY FOR THIS!'

Ethan disappeared around a corner, and Adam slammed himself back on to his bed. His insides were boiling with fury; fury that Ethan could do something so callous and evil; fury with Popularis for not even pointing it out to him; fury at himself for not figuring it out earlier. He'd seen enough films to know that the bad guy was never the obvious suspect. Adam lost it again, screaming at the top of his voice:

'POPULARIS! WHY HAVE YOU DESERTED ME?! YOU'RE MEANT TO HELP M—'

And that's when the printer sprang to life, spitting out page after page of paper, with the same image printed on each page.

Adam stumbled back in surprise. Not because Popularis had appeared when Adam had shouted for it, but because this was the first time Popularis had ever shown up without the blinding flashes and deafening screeches.

Is this your way of throwing a tantrum right back at me? Adam wondered. *Is this your equivalent of storming into my room without knocking?*

Adam plucked one of the pages from his printer and discovered that it was a map. A map that seemed to be pointing to evidence of who the Trojan Idiot might be.

Adam stared at the map in disbelief, then jumped in surprise as two small screens began to glow blindingly bright …

FLASH!

A jolt of electricity kicked him in the brain.

FLASH!

A deafening screech tore at his ears.

FLAAAAAAAASSSSSHHHHH!

Adam opened his eyes to find that, in his room, two screens were glowing unnaturally bright:

1. His old, glitchy phone that Bruce had given him
2. His time-lapse camera that had been filming backstage at the London Arena

And as he investigated each of the items, he discovered that they both contained indisputable evidence of how his friend had betrayed him.

Adam instantly knew what he needed to do. He jumped to his feet, his arms trembling with anticipation as all the pieces of the puzzle began slotting together. He looked at his clock – 01:48 – rather than counting down the days, it was now counting down the *hours and minutes*. Just one hour and forty-eight minutes until his time was up. One hour and forty-eight minutes to gain *eight thousand* new subscribers. One hour and forty-eight minutes to reach one million, or lose all he held dear. And Adam knew exactly how to do it – he was going to make a brand-new video. A *live* video, streaming directly to YouTube. A video that would set everything straight. A video that would simply be titled –

REVENGE.

33

Broken

Knock-knock.

'Adam, I just wanted …'

'Sorry, Callum,' Adam panted as he raced around his room, snatching up everything he would need for his live video. 'Not now. Super-busy.'

'Sorry,' whispered Callum, retreating out of the room.

Adam grabbed his backpack and began filling it with all the equipment he'd need, all the evidence Popularis had shown him – time-lapse camera, map printout, Bruce's old phone.

Knock-knock.

'Sorry, Adam, it's just that …'

'Callum, I mean it,' Adam growled warningly.

'Seriously, buddy, not now.'

Callum backed out of the room again, without a word.

Adam threw his bag over his shoulder, then raced out of his room, only to find Callum standing in the doorway, yet again.

Adam tried to slip past him, but Callum blocked him.

'CALLUM!' Adam barked. 'MOVE!'

'No! Adam! This is important!' Callum insisted as he forced himself into Adam's path.

'CALLUM! I MEAN IT!'

'Adam! Mum said it's really important! I just want to tell you something!'

'WHAT?!'

'I … I'm sorry you didn't get to finish your show.'

'OH MY LIFE, CALLUM! IS THAT IT? THAT'S WHAT YOU'RE WASTING MY TIME FOR? DO YOU REALISE WHAT I'M UP AGAINST RIGHT NOW? I COULD LOSE MY CHANNEL!'

Adam shoved Callum aside and stormed across the landing.

'Wait! That's not all!' Desperate to keep his brother close to him, Callum grabbed hold of Adam's jacket, and growled through gritted teeth – 'Mum told me I had to tell you that … that …'

'TELL ME *WHAT*?!'

Callum looked away and lowered his head.

'That we love you. One million. OK?'

Adam yanked his jacket from Callum's grasp. Callum went stumbling backwards, through Adam's bedroom doorway and straight into Adam's desk. The framed black-and-white photo of their dad

wobbled precariously, then dropped, hitting a wheel on the desk chair with a *SMASH*.

'Yeah, I love you too, Callum,' Adam muttered as he glared at his little brother. '*Minus* one million.'

Adam thundered down the stairs, slammed the front door behind him, then set off at a sprint, to put everything straight.

One hour, forty-two minutes and counting.

34

Fix-up

Adam had escaped the house so fast he didn't look back.

If he had looked back, he might have seen Callum picking the broken pieces of glass from Adam's bedroom floor. He might have seen Callum glancing over the scrap pieces of paper with video plans scribbled on them – ideas, subscriber numbers, some kind of race against time.

He might have seen Callum struggle to make sense of it all, before coming to the conclusion that Adam needed more subs, subs that were required to prevent the loss of his YouTube channel. He might have seen a look of guilt cross Callum's face. Guilt for holding Adam back. For *all* the times he'd held him back. For all the times he'd said 'no' when Adam had asked for help.

It could really help my channel! Adam had said. *Jumping from great heights, little kids in peril ... everyone LOVES that stuff!*

And now, according to the papers on Adam's desk, his channel needed more help than ever. He was in danger of losing the whole thing!

Adam didn't see the look of determination that crossed Callum's face as he set his mind to doing what he thought might help his brother. He didn't see Callum walk slowly and sheepishly to the bottom of the neighbour's garden and stare at the massive oak tree, his body trembling as nerves, adrenalin, and the cold October air attacked him all at once. He didn't see Callum take a deep breath, set his foot to the thick trunk and begin the climb.

He didn't see Callum's arms and legs become streaked with grazes, scrapes and scratches. Every inch of his skin covered in goose bumps as he almost lost his balance several times. His little frame pausing, his breathing steadying. Straddling a branch, taking his phone in hand, pulled from his back pocket, where he'd stored it for safe keeping during the climb.

But if Callum did this right, Adam *would* see what would happen next. Just as everyone who followed his channel would.

Camera on. Recording.

'Hey, guys, it's Callum here,' he said to the camera in a hushed, shaking voice. 'So, I'm kind of doing this as a surprise for Adam. This was a video he really wanted me to film back when we were on holiday in Ibiza, and then again, a few months back, but I kind of chickened out and let him down. So, since he's been having a bit of a rough time lately, I thought maybe this would cheer him up.

'You, err, might be wondering what I'm doing out here in October, in the freezing cold, way up in a massive tree ...' He turned the camera around to capture the almost leafless, moonlit branches all around him, then pointed it downwards to reveal the stomach-turning view below – a back garden a long way down, with a pale blue rectangle in the centre. 'My neighbours told me I'm welcome to use their pool whenever I want. I'm not sure they meant I could jump out of their ten-metre oak tree into it. But they never said I *couldn't*! I'm just hoping this waterproof case for my phone works! So here's the plan ... *wait!*'

Callum suddenly froze, lowering his voice to an urgent whisper. 'Someone's coming!'

Callum twisted himself around on the branch, and pointed the camera down again, this time towards the road behind the O'Bannons' garden.

There, on the pavement below, obscured by a hedge, someone was filming themselves on a phone.

'So, you might be wondering why I've decided to stab my best friend in the back,' the obscured person said to their camera, 'and the answer is simple – he's not a nice guy. All he cares about is subs, money, more subs, more money ... and he's stabbing everyone else in the back just to get those things. He deserves to lose all the fame and popularity he's raked in for himself. He *definitely* deserves to lose his YouTube channel. And if all goes to plan, by the end of the day, he *will*. Operation Justice is underway!'

Callum could not believe
his ears. He had to warn Adam.
To tell him that he was about to
walk into some kind of trap! He
quickly shut his camera off, then went
to call Adam, but the phone slipped from his grasp.

He lunged to catch it.

He reached too far.

He lost his grip ... lost his balance ... And
then ...

Down Callum went. He reached desperately for
a branch. His fingers gripped one, but he was falling
too fast and it was ripped from his grasp, twisting
him around, falling backwards now, reaching again,
but there were no branches left to reach for. Slipping

helplessly through the air, Callum could do nothing but scream. And then. Just like that. His screams came to a sudden end.

Silence.

Darkness.

Cold.

So cold.

Then Callum kicked himself up from the bottom of the pool, launched himself to the surface, filled his lungs with the cool night air and clambered on to the side of the pool. Shivering, shaking, lucky to be alive.

Arms wrapped around himself, pacing back and forth, he didn't seem to know what to do with himself. And then he remembered – his phone! He hunted for it, all around the tree. He had to call Adam! He had to warn him. But his phone was nowhere to be seen, until ... He finally found it. Lots of it. In tiny, shattered pieces at the edge of the pool.

Calling Adam was definitely out of the question. He would have to *find* him instead. But how? *Where?*

Then Callum pulled a piece of paper from his

pocket. A piece of paper he'd picked up from Adam's desk – *a map*. It was soggy and the ink was running, but Callum could just about make out the route it plotted.

'Yes!' Callum exclaimed through chattering teeth.

Then off he ran, as fast as his trembling legs could carry him.

35

Following

'**B**ruce! I need your help!' Adam was running through the streets, massively out of breath, with his phone slammed against his ear. 'I'm making a video. Right now! I need you to meet me at … I don't know … the Worry Tree in Columb's Park, in, like, five minutes!'

Unlike the previous night, Bruce was right there when Adam needed him. And ten minutes later the two of them were running together, through the cold and dark, towards the location marked on Adam's printed map, which he held tight in his fist.

'Adam, listen, about last night – I'm sorry AGAIN I let you down, man,' said Bruce, working up a massive sweat in his mountaineering jacket. 'I didn't explain right, I don't know what happened. I got to the airport and my ticket had been cancelled. I don't get it, I mean—'

'Forget about it, Bruce, I've told you, it wasn't your fault,' Adam breathlessly interrupted. 'None of it was your fault.'

'Thanks, Adam. But ... can you tell me one thing ... *where are we running to?*'

'No time,' Adam panted. 'I'll explain when we get there.'

Adam's brain was spinning in circles as his emotions pulled him back and forth – if it all went to plan this would be his biggest video ever. But if it went wrong ... He didn't even want to think about that. He didn't want to think about anything that wasn't part of his plan. Though he may have liked to know that, not too far away, a breathless figure was closing in on them, about to ruin *everything*.

36

Caught and Captured

Adam and Bruce finally stopped running. They doubled over, hands on knees, fighting for breath as Adam rechecked the location on his map.

'Where now?' asked Bruce, clutching at the stitch in his side.

'We're here,' replied Adam.

'*Here?* This is where we're going to shoot your video?'

'Nuh-uh,' said Adam, straightening up and pointing to the lens of his phone camera that was poking out of his shirt pocket. 'Not where we're *going* to shoot my video. Where we *already are* shooting my video. Live. Streaming. Right now.'

Bruce looked shocked.

'I don't get it. Why? At this manky old garage on the side of the train tracks? *Live?*'

Adam smiled.

'I had a message from Popula— from a friend. They told me to come to this garage. Said I would find something interesting here.'

'Hang on,' laughed Bruce. 'You've sprinted here, in the freezing cold, in the dark, to film a *live* video, of *that* graffiti-covered garage, because your friend told you to, and you don't even know what's *inside* it? Man, you must really trust this friend of yours!'

'Yeah,' Adam chuckled in reply. 'I've never spoken to anyone about this because I was worried I'd sound nuts, but someone's been trying to sabotage my channel. First I thought it was you, then I thought maybe it was Callum being an idiot, then I thought it was you again, then, today, I thought it was Ethan, and ... and that's when my friend got in touch with me again and reminded me about *this* thing ...' Adam pulled a tiny camera, no bigger than a biscuit, from his back pocket and held it up for Bruce to see. 'My time-lapse camera. I set it up last night, backstage at the London Arena. Thought it'd

313

be cool to capture all the behind the scenes stuff. Turns out I captured more than I expected, because while the show was in full swing, someone crept backstage and shut off all the power. Got my show cancelled. Cost the venue hundreds of thousands of pounds. Got the venue investigating a suspected security breach ...'

'Whoa,' Bruce muttered quietly. 'That's like ... yeah. So, did you, er ... see this person's face?'

'Yes, Bruce,' Adam shot back with a stony-faced glare. '*Your* face.'

The two stood there, eyes locked, complete silence, and Adam saw the old Bruce ooze to the surface – rage, anger, hatred bubbling up. He looked as though he might lunge at Adam, but then, glancing at the camera in Adam's pocket, he remembered he was being streamed live on YouTube, and 'friendly' Bruce reappeared.

'Whoa! *What?* Nah, mate. You've been had. What are you even talking about? It must have been face-swapping technology! I see the ads all over the internet. It *wasn't* me, Adam! How could you even think that?!'

'A face-swapping app! Of course! Why didn't I think of that?' Adam laughed, shaking his head as if in embarrassment. And then he stopped. 'Oh, I know. Because he had your *shoes* too! Is there a shoe-swapping app? And your jacket. And your watch. And your rounded shoulders. And the birth-mark on the back of your neck …'

Bruce simply closed his eyes and gave a snort of laughter.

'Adam. Mate. I don't know what you think you captured on that thing, but I'm telling you, it was *not ME!*' Bruce lunged forwards, smacked the camera out of Adam's hand, then stamped on it after it fell clattering to the road.

Adam tried to hide his trembling hands, then he forced a knowing smirk.

'Bruce. Do you honestly think I'm such an idiot that I didn't take the memory card out first?'

Adam kicked himself for being such an idiot that he hadn't taken the memory card out first.

But Adam wasn't done. He had more.

'And then my friend told me to have a search through my old phone – the phone you gave me – and guess what I found? An app, hidden away, deep within the folders. It's called "Remote Access". It lets the owner of the app take complete control of the phone without even touching it. With that app, they can control everything – emails, messages, my YouTube account, even my *banking app* – all from their very own laptop. Even if they're on the other side of the world or, like, if I was in *Ibiza*. At first I couldn't figure out how the app got on there, but then I realised, it was already on there when you gave it to me, wasn't it, Bruce? I thought it was a bit much turning up with your parents like that. You thought you'd use it to mess with me, maybe send fake messages to my friends, pretending to be me, stuff like that. But you didn't know I was going to become a big YouTuber, and when I did, it meant you could mess with me in bigger ways than you'd ever imagined – like accessing my photos to play a video of me when I was onstage at WebCon! Like deleting all my videos when I was in Ibiza. Like stealing all the money from my bank account!'

To Adam's discomfort, Bruce didn't look the least bit worried by any of these accusations. In fact, he was actually *smiling*.

'That all sounds terrible, Adam, it really does,' Bruce chuckled, 'but what makes you think I had anything to do with that stuff?'

'Oh, I don't *think* you did it at all, Bruce. I *know* you did it! I can *prove* you did it! Because guess who that Remote Access app is registered to? That's right, the one and only Bruce Kilter!'

'Well, yeah, it would be wouldn't it?' Bruce said with a carefree shrug. 'I mean, that's *my* phone you're holding! There's no law against having remote access to your own phone. There *is* a law against stealing other people's phones though, Adam. What *are* you doing with *my* phone, Adam? I never gave you that! I've been looking for it for months! I even reported it *stolen*.'

A white-hot panic began to rise in Adam's chest. This was not going to plan at all! He was playing Bruce at his own game and Bruce was winning! But Adam had one more trick up his sleeve, one final blow to take Bruce down; he just hoped this one would work.

'OK, I get it,' said Adam, trying to stay cool. 'You want to pretend you never gave me that phone.

Fine. Let me just show you one more thing …'
Adam held up the map that his printer had churned
out, and he pointed to the address at the big arrow,
right in the centre. 'Fourteen Station Road. That's
where my friend told me to go next. So that's where
we are. That's why we're here.'

Bruce gave another shrug. 'And?'

'And, for the benefit of my viewers, could you
read what it says just underneath the address?'

Bruce leaned forwards, gazed at the map for a
few seconds, then read it out loud.

'"Bruce Kilter, Ford Focus". What's that supposed
to mean?'

'Well, surely that first bit isn't too confusing,
Bruce – it's *your name*. And the second bit is a name
too – the name of a car. The exact make and model
of my *mum's* car, actually, which, as it happens, was
stolen from outside our house, last year.'

'I wouldn't do this if I were you, Adam,' Bruce
warned quietly.

'Well, lucky for me, I'm *not* you,' replied Adam.
'I can't think of anyone I'd rather not be! I'd rather
be a cow's backside than be you, Bruce! I'd rather be

a flea in a monkey's sweaty armpit than be you! Being you is the worst thing I can possibly imagine, and I wouldn't wish it on my own worst en— Oh wait. You *are* my worst enemy.'

'You *really* don't want to do this,' Bruce smirked.

'Tell me, Bruce, what do you think this means – your name, that garage, my mum's car? You don't think my friend was trying to tell me something, do you?'

Adam strolled over to the garage, gripped the handle and gave it a turn.

'Let's see, shall we?'

37

Time to Say Goodbye

Adam made sure his camera was in position. He gripped the handle of the garage door, and began to turn.

'Let's see what's hiding inside, shall we?'

'You really, really don't want to do that, mate,' Bruce growled.

But Adam simply smiled. He turned to Bruce and said, 'Time to say goodbye,' then he yanked on the handle to reveal that ...

The garage was locked.

Adam pulled again. And again. But despite looking like it might fall apart if you so much as blew on it, the garage door did not budge.

Panic coursed through Adam's veins. He hadn't

prepared for this. He *had* to open that garage. He kicked at the handle, the noise drowning out Callum's far-off cries —

'Adam! No! Stop!'

Adam gave one more mighty kick and — *CLANG!* — the handle fell on to the road, and the garage door gave a short, sharp lurch, confirming it was finally unlocked.

Adam's smile grew to a grin. He had Bruce exactly where he wanted him. A quick glance at his YouTube page told him his subs were almost exactly where he wanted them too — 999k and counting.

The events that followed happened so fast that Adam couldn't possibly take it all in —

He threw the garage door up.

He heard a cry from somewhere nearby.

He pointed his phone at the opening door.

He fell backwards in horror when he saw what was really inside the garage —

'Oh, I think you can put that camera down, young man,' smiled Mrs Kilter, sitting in a camping chair inside the garage, alongside her husband.

'You will find that your live stream was actually cancelled before it even began,' Mr Kilter happily added. 'Not to fear though, we've been streaming for you. And that will end forthwith.'

Mr Kilter raised an iPad that had been resting on his lap and revealed a video feed from several hidden cameras surrounding them all. A video feed in which Adam was the star. A video feed that was being streamed live on to Adam's own channel. Mr Kilter then made a big show of pressing the big red 'END STREAM' button on the YouTube App.

'We got everything we needed,' added Bruce. 'All caught on camera – you with your grubby mitts on my *stolen* phone, then you breaking into my parents' garage …'

'I think you can expect another visit from the police, Adam,' Mrs Kilter gleefully informed him.

'Yes,' agreed Mr Kilter, 'and an automatic cancellation of your YouTube channel for streaming a video of yourself committing criminal acts. What a pity.'

'What?' Adam gasped in a whisper of disbelief. '*Why?* Why would you…'

'Why would we do this?' said Mrs Kilter, the fake smile dropping from her face. 'Because we don't believe that stealing is a good thing! We don't think people should get away with it!'

'But I didn't steal Bruce's phone! You know I didn't!'

'Oh, you stupid little child,' Stan Kilter sighed angrily. 'This is about so much more than a silly little phone. This is about my livelihood! My life's work! And what *your jumped-up father* stole from *me* when we were supposed to be *business partners*!'

'Business partners?' Adam scoffed. 'Mum told me you were Dad's *assistant* and he had to fire you because you were trying to sell his computer designs to another company!'

Stan looked momentarily stunned. He coughed nervously, sat up straight and adjusted his jacket.

'Well … I … err… guess that's just another item to add to the colossal list of things that your *ignorant* mother knows NOTHING about!'

Adam felt his cheeks burn bright with rage.

'You don't talk about my mum—' he growled.

'I *beg* your pardon?' shrieked Steph Kilter. 'How *dare* you?! How dare someone like *you* speak to *us* like that?!'

'It's quite all right, darling,' Mr Kilter assured his wife with a hand on her shoulder, 'quite all right. You mustn't let someone so insignificant have such an effect upon you.' Then, to Adam, 'Your father and I worked on that algorithm for *five* years. *Five years!* Then he throws me to the dogs and runs off with *our* design, all to himself, and what does he do with it?

Nothing. Absolutely nothing. That algorithm could have turned my AI business into a multi-billion-pound behemoth! But no, you father, in his unrivalled selfishness, decided *not* to share our work with anyone else. To keep it locked away from the rest of the world! And into his grave he took it! Stubbornly! When so many others could have profited from it!'

Adam just stood there, blinking in disbelief. Then finally he spoke.

'Well, Mr Kilter, firstly, *you* may have worked on Dad's algorithm for five years, but *he* had been working on it his entire life, because it was *his* software to do whatever he wanted with. Secondly, the only people you think could have profited from it – the only people you care about – is *yourselves,* your greedy, selfish, money-grabbing selves. And finally, no matter what kind of beef you had with my dad, picking a fight with a little child like me is hardly the ultimate revenge against him, is it? It's not like you're going to make him angry and regret his decision to fire you – he's *dead*! Did you miss that tiny little detail? You're wasting your time! All three of you!'

Adam expected all three of the Kilters to run at him in an explosion of fury, but, to his huge surprise, they stayed exactly where they were, in complete silence, smirking at each other. And Adam got the distinct impression that they knew something he didn't.

'Revenge?' chuckled Mr Kilter. 'You really think this is about *revenge*? You really don't have a clue, do you? This isn't about getting my own back on some insignificant *corpse,* it's about retrieving what is rightfully mine. It's about taking control of Popularis Incrementum and sending our business positively *stratospheric*!'

Adam's legs went weak beneath him.

'Did you just say *Pop* …'

He couldn't believe what he was hearing.

'Popu …'

Everything began to spin.

'Pop … Popularis is … it's *my dad's* algorithm?'

He felt as if the entire world had been pulled out from beneath him.

'My *dad* designed Popularis Incrementum? It's *his*?'

'No, Adam,' said Bruce. 'You haven't been paying attention, have you? It *was* your dad's, but now it's *my* dad's.'

'And you know about it because ...' Adam was struggling to take it all in.

'Because Stanley helped *invent* it!' Mrs Kilter barked. 'Do keep up!'

'And it's about time it *did come* to me!' added Mr Kilter. 'After all we've been through trying to get our hands on it! Stealing your dad's ridiculous car, hoping there might be some remnants of Popularis in his prototype in-car computer. That was a waste of time! Then taking your mum's rusty old pile of junk ... equally as pointless! And then we gave you that phone and we used it to watch your every move, and ... BINGO! You led us straight to the treasure! We saw Popularis Incrementum in all its glory! And then all we had to do was make you struggle – you see, it's the whole point of the program – it appears to you when you need assistance. So we showed that crowd at your silly Web Convention just what a blithering idiot you really are – *Nappy-ena* indeed. We deleted your videos, we shut down your poor excuse of a show, we emptied your bank ... But Popularis's appearances were not as consistent as I had hoped. In fact, it barely ever showed up when we coaxed it to do so. But even so, we knew it was following you, and if we could trap *you,* then we could trap Popularis. And that's when I came up with the rather ingenious idea of using our Trojan phone to send a map to your printer, in the guise of Popularis. And here you are, right in the palm of our hands. Now all we need is for Popularis to pop up on our iPad, and we'll have it in our grasp. Trapped! It'll be ours forever! And it will be all thanks to you.'

'No.' Adam shook his head, unable to listen to any more. 'You can't. You *can't!*' And then he thought about it and realised he didn't have a thing to worry about. 'You actually *can't,*' he calmly informed them with a wry smile. 'You can't *make* Popularis appear *anywhere.* Not even *I* can! That thing's got a mind of its own. I could call for it all day long and it still wouldn't turn up. You'll never get your hands on it.'

'Well,' said Mr Kilter with a smirk, 'that's where

we've been paying more attention than you …'

Mrs Kilter got out of her chair, tugged on a huge brown tarp from behind her, and revealed Adam's mum's missing car.

Inside Adam's pocket, the clock on his phone was counting down, just like his alarm clock. Except the numbers were no longer counting down the days, hours or minutes until his time was up – they were counting down the *seconds*.

Reach one million … or lose all you hold dear

10

9

8

'You see,' continued Mr Kilter, 'we've discovered a pattern.'

All three Kilters climbed inside the car.

'And we found that we can now predict, with perfect accuracy, exactly when Popularis will appear,' he called from the open window as he started the car, the engine revving with a high-pitched squeal and a mashing of gears.

'Adam!' came Callum's voice from one of the various, maze-like side streets nearby. 'Adam, it's a trap! Get out of there!'

The noise of the car engine drowned out Callum's cries.

'There is one action that will coax the algorithm to reveal itself *every single* time,' Stan hollered. 'It rears its head, without fail, whenever you or one of your family … is about to get hurt.'

Stan gunned the car. It shot out of the garage, across the cobbled streets, directly towards Adam.

Callum raced out from a side street, desperate to warn Adam.

'CALLUM! NO!' Adam screamed, but it was all too late –

Callum didn't notice the old Ford Focus thundering towards him.

The Kilters didn't notice Callum darting out in front of them.

There was no blinding flash from a screen.

No deafening screech tearing at Adam's ears.

No reaching one million.

38

Flash

The voices were desperate and panicked. Bodies pushed and shoved this way and that. Someone barked orders, but Adam didn't hear them. He was barged aside, but he didn't feel it. His head swirled like the blue lights that strobed through the window – *flash – flash – flash*. The vehicle lurched around a corner and Adam's phone fell from his pocket, but he didn't notice. It clattered to the ground. The foot of a paramedic cracked the screen clear in two. One side of the break reflected Callum's limp arm as it dangled over the side of the stretcher as if lifelessly reaching out for help. The other side remained a perfectly working window to all that Adam held dear – his subs were steadily creeping towards one million, but it was too late, the count-down was over. The deadline was up. Adam had failed.

The heart rate monitor hooked up to Callum's finger was steadily creeping towards zero.

Adam looked down at his phone. Then back to the screen of the heart monitor. Then back to his phone. A keeling dizziness overtook him. A series of images swam through Adam's mind – one screen after another, message after message:

- The hotel TV screen – *Don't lose Callum*.
- His camera screen – *Go with your brother*.
- *Express yourself*
- *Reach one million* …
- … *or lose all you hold dear.*

A door opened up inside Adam's brain and a flood of realisation came pouring in – not a single one of those messages had been a suggestion for a video. He realised that now. They were *warnings*! Warnings about his *life*. About *Callum's* life.

Adam was aware of two sensations echoing through his mind – his dad's voice in his ear, *Love you one million*, *buddy* and the small hand in his, which he held so dear.

'That's what Popularis meant!' he whispered to himself. 'It was never about one million *subs*. It was my *dad's* One Million that I needed to grow to! And my *channel* isn't the thing I hold most dear! I don't even *care* about my channel! *This* is what I hold dear! Callum! Mum! Ethan! *Us!* I was so focused on myself. On my goals … I didn't realise I already had exactly what I want … what I need. I was so selfish! I was lost. And now I'm losing it all! And now …'

'Popularis?' Adam managed to summon the word from his numb lips. His voice like nails scraping on stone. 'You can fix this, right?'

He looked to his phone, but it didn't flash an answer. It simply continued counting his oh so important subs: 999,211 … 999,219 … 999,233 …

He looked to the screen of the heart monitor.

'Popularis, you *are* going to fix this, right?' he asked again. Anger and determination gritted his words, like rocks scraping together.

But Popularis wasn't in that screen either. It

simply counted down the beats of Callum's ever-slowing heart – 22 … 21 … 19 …

Adam was suddenly on his feet.

'YOU CAN FIX THIS!' The words burst out of him like boulders smashing against a rock face. 'YOU CAN FIX THIS! YOU SAVED ME BEFORE! YOU SAVED MUM! NOW YOU CAN SAVE CALLUM! SAVE CALLUM! SAVE HIIIMMMMMM!'

'We're doing all we can, OK?' replied a paramedic, gently pushing Adam back into the ambulance's fold-down seat. 'But we need you to stay in your seat and try to keep calm.'

Adam watched on in dismay as two shiny paddles were lifted from the wall. A tiny, high-pitched mechanical scream grew louder and louder. The paddles were pressed against Callum's chest. Adam reached for his brother's small hand.

'CLEAR!'

FLASH!

A jolt of electricity kicked him in the brain.

FLASH!

A deafening screech tore at his ears.

FLAAAASSSSHHH!

Adam's entire world was one big, blinding light.

He felt himself falling, spinning, tumbling out of control. Adam fell through nothingness, plunging deeper and deeper, spiralling out of control …

Adam continued falling, twisting, plummeting …

A water slide of emotions yanked him left, right and centre; faster and faster he fell.

Suddenly, the chaos began to settle, the twisting vivid vortex of memories had come to an end, everything went quiet. And as the blinding light began to ebb away, like ripples in water, he landed with a thump.

39

Introduction

Adam's dad smiled up at him from the framed black-and-white photo on Adam's desk. It was a smile that usually seemed full of warmth and reassurance for Adam, but right now it felt more like it was full of questions.

Adam stumbled backwards in shock.

Where are the paramedics?

Where's the ambulance?

Where's CALLUM?

How did I get here?

Adam was standing in the middle of his bedroom, his old computer staring at him, with a single line of text across the screen —

My name is Popularis Incrementum, and I

am an AI that will solve all your problems. Trust me.

'I don't get it,' whispered Adam. 'What's going on? What happened to Callum?'

Feverish with panic, dizzy with confusion, Adam looked around at his room. Nothing was making sense. There was no sign of his new phone. No giant TV. His bedroom, his old computer, his old desk, his old phone ... Everything was just as it had been one year earlier.

'What is going on here? WHAT! IS! GOING! ON?!'

Adam collapsed into his desk chair as a hinge suddenly went in his anglepoise lamp, causing it to swivel and literally shine a spotlight on him. Then, from downstairs, a radio was flicked on, blaring out a song – *Nowhere to run, nowhere to hide, nowhere to run to, baby!*

And then Adam realised –

'I've lived all of this before!'

The message on the monitor changed.

OK, I don't have all day. I'm a busy AI. Either click, or don't.

A countdown was ticking away in the bottom corner of the screen – *7 ... 6 ... 5 ...*

His mouse hovered over the link.

'Popularis?' Adam whispered. 'I don't get it. What's happening?'

But as Adam thought about it, he wondered if, actually, maybe he *did* get it – Popularis *had* helped him before with the bike stunt, the balcony fall, his mum getting out of that taxi, by slowing things down, speeding things up, even putting things on pause, so maybe ...

'Popularis ...' Adam whispered. 'Did you hit ... *rewind?* Are you giving me a *second chance* to get this right?'

KNOCK! KNOCK!

A small head poked through the doorway.

'Adam, can you just ... ?'

'CALLUM!'

Adam leaped from his chair. He flew across his room and swept Callum up into his arms, hugging him so tight Callum could barely breathe.

'Wow,' croaked Callum. 'You *really* wanna help with my homework!'

'Yes!' Adam laughed through his tears. 'More than *anything*!'

'OK … Well … if you, err … quit it with the soppy cuddles for a sec, I'll go get it.'

Adam hid his tears with laughter as Callum ran off to his room, then came back with his project – 'An Interview with Your Hero', to which Callum had added his subtitle: 'My Brother, Adam'. And that was it. It was too much. Adam was a sobbing, blubbering, snotty mess who wouldn't let go of his little brother's hand.

'What is *wrong* with you?' Callum laughed.

But soon enough, Adam's tears became contagious, and Callum too dissolved into a sobbing, blubbering, snotty mess, and he didn't even know *why*! And then Mum came up to see what the problem was, and before she knew it, she was scooped up into one big sobbing, blubbering, snotty group hug that went on far too long for you to bother reading about.

And there, on Adam's desk, the Popularis timer had run down to zero. No spell. No deadline. No mess.

40

Here We Go Again

It was way past Callum's bedtime, but it was totally worth staying up for — Adam had come up with the idea to make Callum's homework a video interview, rather than a written one, and despite only having a half-dead phone and an ancient computer to film and edit on, the final result was a masterpiece.

'When did you learn all this stuff?' Callum's eyes were sparkling. 'When did your videos get so *pro*?!'

'Pretty cool, huh?' agreed Adam. 'What do you say tomorrow we set up our own YouTube channel?'

'Are you flarting *serious*?! That'll be *awesome*! Just you and me!'

'And maybe Ethan can help out from time to time,' suggested Adam.

'Yes! It's what you've always wanted to do! It's going to be *awesome*! Except –' Callum's grin began to diminish – 'do you think I'll be any good? Like, I'm not too boring, am I? You know, too normal.'

'Callum, you are just like the rest of us – a perfectly normal bottle of Coke and a very average pack of Mentos.' Adam mimed a volcanic eruption, and Callum's grin returned, bigger than ever.

'But let's start by just uploading a few of our older videos, yeah?' added Adam.

'Oh, man,' said Callum, with a mischievous chuckle, 'I know exactly which one we should upload first!'

'Right there with ya!' Adam was laughing so hard at the thought of re-uploading the 'Glue Shampoo' video that he didn't hear Callum singing 'Heyyy Nappy-rena!' under his breath.

'How many subs do you think we could get?' wondered Callum.

'Doesn't really matter.' Adam shrugged. 'But if

we ever make any money from it, the first thing we're doing is getting Mum a new gearbox.'

'Deal. Wait … *what*? You can make *money* on YouTube? How much?'

'Callum, trust me, if all you focus on is numbers and figures and trying to win the internet, then you've already lost.'

'Like *you* would know,' groaned Callum as the sound of their mum's footsteps came thumping up the stairs and he quickly slunk out of Adam's room before he got caught out of bed.

Too late …

'Callum!' his mum snapped. 'Bed! Now!'

'I was just saying goodnight to Adam!'

'Well, say goodnight to Adam, quickly, then get yourself into bed.'

'Night night, Adam!' said Callum, poking his head into Adam's room and giving a dramatically over-the-top wave.

'Night, Callum!' Adam called back, with an equally dramatic wave. 'Sleep tight!'

After Mum had finished shooing Callum back into his room, she poked her head in to check on

Adam and found him staring at the framed photo of his dad, which he had plucked from his desk and was cradling in his hands.

'You OK now?' she asked gently.

'NIGHT NIGHT, ADAM!' Callum called again, purposely trying to wind up his mum.

'Yeah,' Adam told her as he laughed softly through his nose. 'I don't predict any more snot and tears for at least another twelve minutes.'

'Ooh, so I'm safe to come in?' Mum giggled with exaggerated excitement.

'For now, yeah.' Then, 'NIGHT, CALLUM!'

So in she went and perched on the edge of his bed.

'I—' she began, but was interrupted by yet another cry from Callum's room.

'NIGHT, ADAM!'

'Oh my life. A whirlwind of annoyingness, right, Mum?' chuckled Adam. 'NIGHT, CALLUM! SWEET DREAMS!'

'I was going to say,' his mum continued with a sigh and a smile, 'that I love that old picture of your dad.'

'That's the weird thing – I was just thinking exactly the opposite. Of all the pictures we've got of Dad, I have no idea why I have this one. It's old and smudged, it was taken before I was even born and looks like it was torn out of a thirty-year-old newspaper.'

'You have it because, last year, I found it in a box of stuff from his old office, and when I asked you if you wanted it you said "yes". And the reason it looks like it was torn out of an old newspaper is because it *was* torn out of an old newspaper. Not thirty years ago though. Fourteen years ago. The year you were born.'

'Well, I'm going to replace it with a new one, with all four of us in it,' said Adam, opening up the frame and removing the picture from inside. He unfolded the newspaper page to read the article headline – 'Internet Wizard Invents Algorithm to Predict Your Thoughts.'

'It's so weird that he used to be this computer nerd celebrity, way back.'

'Way back?' Mum scoffed. 'They still study his papers in some universities!'

'NIGHT, ADAM!' came another yell from Callum's room.

'Oh my life, GOODNIGHT, CALLUM!'

'GO TO SLEEP!' added Mum, rolling her eyes in tired despair. 'YOU'RE NOT FUNNY!'

Adam proceeded to open up the newspaper page even further, to get a proper read of the article, but something caused him to freeze in astonishment.

'Oh no ... you're not going to blow again, are you?' Mum joked, picking up Adam's pillow to use as a shield in case of a blub-fest emergency. 'You told me I had twelve minutes!'

She tousled his hair lovingly, then gave his forehead a tender kiss before quietly slipping out of the room, leaving Adam alone with his thoughts.

But Adam paid her no attention. He was too dumbstruck by the part of the photograph that had been folded over to fit it into the frame – a small section of office, just over his dad's shoulder: a desk, a lamp, a younger Stan Kilter carrying a tray of coffee cups, an ancient computer, which Adam recognised as the exact same one that was sat on his

own desk at that very minute... and on that screen was just two words. Two words, which probably meant nothing to anyone else, but to Adam meant everything –

Popularis Incrementum

What was it all about? Adam whispered in *his* mind. *Why did he invent it, then do nothing with it? It really feels like he programmed it to give me advice even after he was gone! But ... but it was so much more than that!*

Those tricks it did ... they weren't to make my videos look cool ... they ... they ... they saved my life. It was ...

The computer screen flickered.

Words began to appear.

So. Did you learn your lesson?

'I ... I *think so*,' Adam muttered. 'Grow to one million by this time next year ... Do it not, and lose all you hold dear. You weren't talking about subs, were you?'

More words appeared on the screen.

You're doing it again, talking to a computer program. Popularis is designed to predict your questions, but it is NOT alive. I am not alive, Adam. I'm sorry. But I DO love you. Always. To one million.

'Wait!' Adam pleaded. 'I just need to know one thing ...'

The answer to your next question is simple – twelve bananas and a cup of sugar.

'That ... has nothing to do with what I was going to ask.'

Or blue. Possibly penguins. I have to admit I'm a little stumped here. Chocolate cheesecake?

'Wait! I just want to know ...'

This session has expired. My purpose has been fulfilled. Farewell, Adam Beales. I shall go now. But I won't be leaving you.

The screen went blank and Adam had a feeling that Popularis wouldn't be visiting him again. Adam smiled. Blub-fest part two was definitely on the way, but he was managing to hold it back, for now, while he tried to wrestle with everything that had just happened.

The idea that his dad had sent him messages from beyond the grave to give him advice on making *YouTube videos* now seemed embarrassingly laughable to Adam. But maybe he shouldn't be embarrassed. Maybe, he wondered, he was supposed to get it wrong, and only then could he figure out how to do it the right way – not making videos – *living his life*, being a part of his family. And maybe, he thought, his dad *did* live on – not in the internet – but in Adam, and in his mum, and in Callum ...

Adam decided that, first thing the next day, he

was going to do all the things his dad used to do. He was going to get the drill and the screwdriver and he was finally going to put his new TV … no, wait, he didn't own that new TV yet, not for another six months! He would screw *something* to the wall. *Anything!* He would do crazy-leg dancing to Stevie Wonder in the kitchen; he would race as Baby Peach in *Mario Kart* all the time; he would catch the spiders – he would do *all* of it. He wouldn't be disrespecting his dad's memory, as though he were taking his place, he would be *honouring* his dad's memory, as if his dad was living on in him. And there was one thing he didn't have to wait until tomorrow to do …

'HEY, CALLUM?' he yelled as he leaned back and spun himself in his chair.

'YEAH?' Callum yelled back.

'NIGHT NIGHT!'

'NIGHT, ADAM!'

'AND, CALLUM?'

'YEAH?'

'LOVE YOU, ONE MILLION!'

And there it was. As simple as that. Adam had

grown to one million. And he knew that he wouldn't make the same mistake again – no selfishness, no obsessing about popularity, no putting his family second – this time he was going to keep a tight grip on all he held dear.

I get to do it all again, thought Adam, *and this time I'll do it right.*

The chance to get to live the year all over again felt like the greatest gift Adam could imagine. Well ... at least it *did* until he realised it wasn't all good news ...

'I hope you've done your homework, Adam!' his mum called up the stairs. 'You've got *HISTORY* tomorrow!'

Adam smiled and opened his busted-up old phone.

Compose text

22.32 from Adam:

Hey Buddy, any idea what Snidren's homework is tomorrow? Feels like a year since he set it!

22.32 from Ethan:

OMG! I totally forgot! No idea! I think it was something to do with the Romans? Or the Egyptians? No! World War II! Or ... definitely something to do with the olden days.

We're so getting detention aren't we.

22.33 from Adam:

DEFINITELY! It will not be fun. Glad I won't be suffering it on my own! You're a good friend Ethan. And hey, me and Callum are gonna start making amazing YouTube vids after school tomorrow. They'll be even more awesome if you can join us! Let me know in the morning. Off to bed now. See you tomorrow!

x

(delete x)

Send ...

Adam had finally finished worrying about facing another day of old Bruce's school bullying, and was just on the verge of sleep when his banged-up old phone buzzed from beside his pillow. And when he picked it up ... *CONFUSION OVERLOAD!*

There, on his screen, was a message – a message from Bruce – a message he had already received, *ten months ago*. No ... not ten months ago. *In two months' time!* A message from ... *the future!*

'*Hey, Adam, we got cut off just now, so I thought I'd send you a vid, just to make sure you got the message ...*'

Adam hit pause. This didn't make any sense! It was the video Bruce had sent him just after he'd received his WebCon award, except ...

'This hasn't happened yet!' Adam whispered. 'It's not possible!'

He pressed play again.

'*Anyway, just wanted to wish you luck. I found your category on the WebCon Twitter feed, and saw you were up for an award ...*'

Adam stared at the screen, baffled beyond belief. There was future Bruce, in his huge house, with his gigantic TV, and the driveway full of cars outside the window, and …

Wait!

Adam thought he saw something …

Cars.

He paused the video and zoomed in.

CARS!

He zoomed in even further, and there it was – sat directly between a Chrysler and a BMW, in plain view for Adam to see – the first car that had been stolen from them, back before Mum had had to buy the gearbox banger, the car that his dad had built with his own hands – *the Dadmobile!*

The Kilters had the nerve – no, the *stupidity* – to keep it on their driveway after they'd stolen it!

To get that car back would be like having a bit of his dad returned to him! To get it back would mean never having to use the gearbox banger again!

To get it back … Adam had the perfect plan.

Within seconds he began editing Bruce's video. Transforming it. Chopping it up, moving bits around, zooming in, adding effects, laying down music … and just minutes later, Adam was reclining in his chair, admiring his finished masterpiece.

The screen is black.

Fade in to see Bruce, strolling leisurely through his living room. Classical music plays gently in the background — 'Hey, Adam,' he says to the camera. 'I found your ca——' PAUSE! EXTREME CLOSE-UP ON THE WINDOW! HANDWRITING SCRIBBLES ACROSS THE SCREEN TO ANNOUNCE —

MY DAD'S MISSING CAR!!!
HE FOUND IT!!!!!!

THE MUSIC BURSTS TO LIFE! BOOM! FIREWORK EFFECTS! FLASHING ARROWS! AN EXPLOSION OF BALLOONS! ZOOM IN – ZOOM OUT – ZOOM IN – ZOOM OUT! BOOM! BOOM! BOOM! BOOM! PARTY! PARTY! PARTY!

Adam put the video on loop, posted it on every social media platform imaginable, with the simple heading – 'Bruce Kilter! My hero! Can't wait to get our car back!' And then he tagged every single person he could think of – Bruce, Ethan, everyone at school, the local news, the police …

Nine minutes and fifty-eight seconds later, Adam heard two sounds that told him everything he needed to know –

1. His mum's cheering, squealing and 'Oh my goodness!'ing downstairs told him that the Dadmobile had been returned.
2. The voices outside Adam's window told him exactly who had returned it. 'Alice, we had *no idea* it was yours, obviously.' Mrs Kilter lied through her teeth when Adam's mum opened the door. 'I. Am. *Mortified*. Stan bought it at auction a couple of years ago – a reputable auction house, I might add – and we never *dreamed* it could have been stolen! Anyway, someone alerted us that it was yours, and we immediately brought it straight back to you, completely free of charge!'

But Mrs Kilter's happy, shiny voice was nowhere to be heard when Adam listened to her heading back to Mr Kilter's Bentley, along with Bruce. 'I can't believe you sent *that* video, with *that* car in, to the *very* person we stole it from!' Bruce's mum was hissing furiously as she marched Bruce down the garden path.

'It's not true though!' Bruce insisted as he climbed into the car. 'I never made that video! I've never sent that freak a message in my life!'

Adam could hear Mr and Mrs Kilter yelling at Bruce even when their car was halfway down the street. Then he closed his window and lay back in his bed with a very satisfied grin on his face.

This new year – new *life* – was getting off to a very good start. No more old banger. No more broken gearbox. No more taking any of Bruce's bullying. This time around, everything was going to be different. This time around ...

'Hang on,' Adam said out loud to his empty bedroom. 'Where did that future message even come from? Popularis, I thought you said you weren't coming back!'

But there was no reply.

Adam wondered if Popularis was somewhere else, maybe on the other side of the world, helping some other kid learn the biggest lesson of their life.

And then, down the hallway, as Callum was quietly tapping away on his computer, hoping Mum wouldn't catch him out of bed again, he began searching the internet for a very specific question when a strange-looking advert appeared on his screen. Callum followed the on-screen instructions, and then his screen began to glow so bright he toppled straight off his chair and landed on his bedroom floor with a CRASH.

Adam could see the glowing light even from his room, but as fast as he scrambled out of bed and down the hall, he didn't manage to get to Callum before –

FLASH!

A jolt of electricity kicked Callum in the brain.

FLASH!

A deafening screech tore at his ears.

FLAAAASSSSHHH!

'Callum!' Adam panted, doubled over in Callum's bedroom doorway. 'Please tell me that was not Popularis Incrementum?!'

'Relax!' Callum laughed sheepishly as he picked himself off the floor. 'It was nothing! Unless you really think some stupid internet ad could actually *solve all of my problems*!'

Adam bashed his forehead into Callum's bedroom door. 'Oh no,' he groaned. 'Here we go again …'

Acknowledgements

Adam couldn't have won the internet without all the amazing family, friends and colleagues I have around me. Without such a supportive network group, this book would simply not exist. Surrounding myself with positive people who challenge and guide me daily enabled me to create an absolute BANGER of a story that I hope you all love!

Firstly Mum and Dad. Although they got a mention at the front of the book, it's only right I acknowledge them here too — otherwise I won't get dinner tonight, LOL! However, behind every young child who believes in themselves is a parent who believed in them first. Thanks for believing/supporting/loving me, Mum and Dad. I love you both!

Next up my (not-so-little) brother, Callum. Our relationship is like no other. At times I feel like his parent and at other times I'm sure he feels like mine. However, our bond is magical and I couldn't have asked for a better best friend and brother in one. His comedy, mischievousness and all-round quirkiness gave me a lot of inspiration for the book. He's truly a little/BIG legend. Love you, little bro!

Oran O'Carroll (my Chris) — the man with the deepest voice and the closest eyes to a phone screen that I've ever known. The same man who saw something in me when a lot of others didn't. The same man I look up to as a big brother. And the same man who keeps pushing me daily to constantly evolve and improve. He's the wizard behind the curtain and has made me believe anything is possible, ever since Day One.

James Wills and Tom Clempson. Your support throughout this writing process has been nothing short of astounding! You both kept me right at every turn and helped me shape the book into the fantastic adventure that it now is.

Hannah and the entire Bloomsbury team, especially Emily, Alesha, Fliss, Anna, Jess, Jadene and Mike. What can I say? I've never met a more enthusiastic, passionate and positive bunch of people in my entire life. I can never thank you enough for the support and belief you have in me and my story. Thanks for the advice along the way. You've made this journey as a debut author a very exciting one. And it's a journey I'm glad to have shared with you.

To James Lancett for bringing Adam to life! Being able to visually capture all the different emotions/thoughts/moments within the book was so important to me – and James never failed to deliver! The creativity and talent he has poured into the illustrations are just mind-blowing. I'm jealous of his drawing skills! Teach me your ways, James!!!

To Dom. Thanks for helping me find myself and for always being by my side – through the highs and lows. You will always be my home and you have my whole heart. I love to love you.

To my grandparents. Thanks for your wisdom and advice always. You mean the world to me. Love you both.

To Calum (my Ethan) for being my Day One. You've had my back more times than your knee popped out. You've stuck with me through thick and thin – particularly times when it was uncool to hang around with (that) 'YouTube guy'.

To ~~Joanne and Lee~~ – sorry I mean Joe Tasker and Lee Hinchcliffe. You're the closest friends I've had the pleasure to meet in this crazy 'YouTube-sphere'. Thanks for being two gents and for always being there for a silly FaceTime call.

To my primary seven teacher, Mr McCrossan, for having the patience to read my continuous flow of self-written stories proudly presented on PowerPoint. Your encouragement has meant more than you'll ever know.

And finally to the teachers who believed in me at St Columb's College. I just wanted to say thank you.

Exclusive Q and A!

Adam's real-life little bro, Callum B, has got some burning questions to ask ...

Hi, Adam, I've got a few questions for you about things your readers might want to know, so I hope you're going to give me some good, honest answers!

Of course, fire away!

Right then, let's get started. First of all, can you tell us what your favourite book was when you were younger?

I *loved* the Skulduggery Pleasant series by Derek Landy when I was growing up. I remember getting so excited when the book arrived in our school library and I was the first person to borrow it!

And if you could be any character, from *any* book, who would you be?

Skulduggery Pleasant, obvs! I love his sarcastic and humorous one-liners, and how he uses them to diffuse tense situations! Also, Skulduggery's adventures are filled with action, magic and danger. He faces off against formidable foes and uses his quick thinking and magical abilities to save the day – much like Adam in his adventures with the internet.

So you love to read, but what made you want to *write* a book?

When lockdown happened, I wanted to give myself a project. I had the idea of encapsulating some of my YouTube experiences into a novel, and so writing *Adam Wins the Internet* was my lockdown baby. And I'm very proud of it.

What was it that gave you the idea for *Adam Wins the Internet*?

My journey to becoming a YouTuber in real life was a pretty wild one, so I wanted to write about that, but to give it a magical twist as well as add in a whole bunch of funny moments that happened only in my mind. And also the importance of family in my life.

When you were working on the book, what was your favourite chapter to write and why?

Probably the first one, because I was so excited to start writing my story. I remember the daunting feeling of opening up a new Word document on my computer and typing out 'Chapter 1'. However, the excitement made any sort of intimidation fizzle away because I desperately wanted to share these crazy stories in my head.

The illustrations in the book are brilliant, and really funny. What's your favourite one and why?

I think the illustration where Mum gets covered in Coke from the Mentos prank.

Ha-ha, that's a great one! So, Adam, can you tell us how long you've wanted to be a writer for?

Ever since Primary 7. You'll see at the end of this book I acknowledge my Primary 7 teacher, Mr McCrossan. I loved writing horror stories when I was little. I always sent Mr McCrossan my stories and he would, without fail, give me feedback on what I'd written. That whole process gave me an even bigger appetite for storytelling.

So do you *really* have a magical algorithm at home that helps you with your YouTube videos?

I wish! Ha-ha! Or maybe I do?!

Hmm, fascinating! In the book, Adam gets covered in slime when his radio-controlled octopus malfunctions. Have you ever been slimed in real life?

Lots of times! More than I can count!! Whether it's for a YouTube video, television show or just a revenge prank from you, you little menace – slime and I go *way* back.

Out of all the things you've achieved in your life so far, what are you most proud of?

Proving our parents right when they supported me in my journey on YouTube, and having the opportunity to surprise them with the house of their dreams.

And what do you hope readers will take away from Adam's adventures in the book?

That, above everything, the one thing that truly matters in life is family.

And finally, do you have any advice for those kids out there who want to be a YouTuber like you?

Record videos you like to record. Don't force yourself to record and edit content you're not happy with. Find an interest and film around that. I love playing pranks on my family – so I make lots of videos about that, LOL.

Yeah, I'm well aware of that, thanks very much!

OK – quick-fire round:

- Cats or dogs? **Dogs – of course!**
- Chocolate or sweets? **Sweets**
- Snow or sun? **Sun (even though I glow bright neon pink when I'm in the sun)**
- A day full of adventure or a midnight feast? **Day full of adventure!**
- Burger or chips? **Chips**
- Maths or English? **Maths**
- Mum or Dad? **Bailey (my dog)**

Can't believe you found a way to dodge that question. I was going to use it to blackmail you (mwah-ha-ha!).

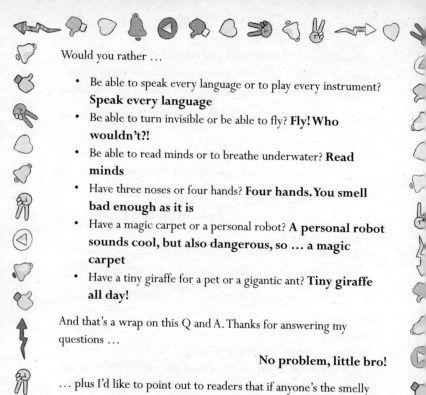

Would you rather …

- Be able to speak every language or to play every instrument?
  Speak every language
- Be able to turn invisible or be able to fly? **Fly! Who
  wouldn't?!**
- Be able to read minds or to breathe underwater? **Read
  minds**
- Have three noses or four hands? **Four hands. You smell
  bad enough as it is**
- Have a magic carpet or a personal robot? **A personal robot
  sounds cool, but also dangerous, so … a magic
  carpet**
- Have a tiny giraffe for a pet or a gigantic ant? **Tiny giraffe
  all day!**

And that's a wrap on this Q and A. Thanks for answering my
questions …

No problem, little bro!

… plus I'd like to point out to readers that if anyone's the smelly
one around here, it's Adam.

What?! Lies! You can't trust a word Callum says.

Now he's WON THE INTERNET,

what's next for

ADAM?

ADAM DESTROYS THE INTERNET

COMING OCTOBER 2023

Read on for a sneak peek of ADAM B's second magical,

heart-warming, record-smashing adventure ...

It was a regular Saturday afternoon, just like any other. Not too hot, not too cold, just … you know, *normal*. And Adam was just a regular thirteen-year-old boy. Not blessed with superpowers, but not totally evil or intent on taking over the world either, just … you know, *normal*. And currently Adam was in a normal pair of skis, racing down a normal glass roof on one of London's tallest normal skyscrapers. For Adam – Internet Sensation Extraordinaire – this was a fairly normal day.

But it wasn't going to stay that way for much longer.

'WOO-HOO!' Adam cheered as he picked up so much speed that he nearly caused a peregrine falcon to have a heart attack as he zoomed past. 'I have no idea how fast I'm going,' Adam bellowed at the camera that was attached to his helmet, 'but I would estimate that I am travelling at a speed of, approximately … *very, very fast*!'

Then just up ahead he saw something that caused his eyes to widen in alarm. His heart began to race. His visor began to fill with sweat. And his voice trembled as he announced to the millions of viewers who were watching him live on YouTube –

'Erm, guys? I can see the edge of the roof now and ... I don't think I can stop!'

Adam was right. He couldn't. At the speed he was pelting down the slope, not even a brick wall would have been able to stop him. But stopping wasn't part of the plan. Adam knew that better than anyone! After all, this whole video was *his* idea. But *planning* to ski off the top of a skyscraper and *actually doing it* are two very different things. And Adam was beginning to wish he'd never come up with such a stupid idea.

'I'm beginning to wish I'd never come up with such a stupid idea!' he screamed at his helmet-cam.

It wasn't even the 'skiing-off-the-top-of-a-skyscraper' thing that scared Adam the most. That was the *easy* bit. It was what was going to happen afterwards that had him quaking in his ski boots. But it was too late for a change of heart now. It was a matter of seconds until he would be hurtling off the edge.

Adam looked directly into the camera and addressed his viewers like a man who was speaking at his own funeral.

'Before I do this, I just have one last thing to tell you. To my mum, to my little brother, Callum, to all of you who have supported me as a YouTuber, I'd just like to say … WHOOOAAA-ARRRGHHH-EEEEEEEE-YEEEEUUUURRRRGHHHH-MMMMUUUUMMMMYYYY!!!!'

Adam shot from the roof.

He soared through the crisp blue air.

He flew towards the helicopter that hovered ahead, towards the trapeze that dangled below it, reaching out towards the outstretched arms of Callum, who was dangling upside down from the trapeze by his knees, and Adam knew, without a doubt, that their hands were never going to meet. He was going to miss Callum by just a few millimetres, and then … ! Adam couldn't even bear to think about it.

But he didn't have to, because – *SMACK*! Adam's hands closed around Callum's wrists! Callum's hands closed around Adam's! Adam looked up into his little brother's eyes and screamed with joy – 'CALLUM! WE DID IT!'

And that's when Callum's legs slipped and Adam

and Callum Beales, stars of their own famous YouTube channel, plummeted towards the cold, hard concrete of the London street far below …

But the brothers didn't scream or cry, or go an exciting shade of green, they just stayed like that – arms linked, eyes locked, breathing as one, in perfect unison as they fell. Then together they shouted –

'Three … two … one …'

Like a meticulously rehearsed dance, they released each other's arms, drifted apart from one another, pulled at the handles that dangled from their chests, and – *WHOOOOMPH*! Their parachutes deployed, and calmly and peacefully they drifted down to the street below, where they were met by the cheers and screams of the thousands of fans lining the pavements, all clamouring to get over the barriers that separated them from the paramedics, security teams and reporters who were rushing to meet Adam and Callum as they removed their parachutes.

But someone else got to the brothers first.

'YES!' whooped Ethan, Adam's best friend, as he congratulated them with a pair of almighty high-fives before breaking into one of his million-mile-an-hour speeches. 'You should have seen yourselves up there! Adam, you were like "*WHOOSH!*" and Callum, you were like "I got this!" and then it was like "Whoa!" and then I thought for sure that you were both gonna die, and then it was like "Yes! They're alive!" and then it was like "No! They're gonna die again! It's gonna be so gross and sticky!" and then it was like "Ahhhh" and then it was like "ARRRRGHHHH!" and then it was like "Doo-di-doo-di-doo, we're just here, floating around in our parachutes like a pair of absolute LEGENDS!" and then it was like "Touchdown!" and then I was running over to you and I was like "YES!" and "High-five!" and "You should have seen yourselves up there!" And I was like, "Adam, you were like '*WHOOSH!*'" And then …'

'Ethan!' Adam interrupted. 'We get it! It was amazing! Thank you! We couldn't have done it without you!'

A peanut flew through the air then bounced off Adam's forehead. They all ignored it.

'Seriously?!' Ethan said. 'Because I didn't really do anything. I just kind of stood around and watched, and then I ate some of those crisps over there, where that guy dressed as a cheetah is them giving away, and then I went over to that lady dressed as an alligator to get one of those blue drinks that she's handing out, and it wasn't bad, but probably a bit too blue for me. Do you think it'll make my pee blue? Because—'

'Ethan!' Adam interrupted again as another peanut hit him. In the nose this time. 'Ouch! Look, Ethan, just knowing you were down here supporting us was all we needed.'

'You actually mean that?'

'Of course I mean that. Now, please can you do me a favour? You see over there? Bruce Kilter, the biggest bully the world has ever seen, standing on top of that bin? Holding up a sign that says "ADAM BEALES IS A MORON"? Well, would you mind getting security to take it off him? Or make him get off the bin? Or ask him to leave or something?'

'Why can't school bullies just stay in school?' Ethan lamented. 'Why do they have to bully us from other places too? Like street corners, and car parks, and ... bins.'

'Yargh!' Adam yelped as a peanut flew directly into his ear.

'Also, Ethan,' Adam added before Ethan could depart on his mission, 'If you could get him to stop lobbing peanuts at us, that would be a really good thing!'

About the Author
and Illustrator

Adam B is a household name. Not only hugely popular online, with his videos boasting over half a billion views overall, Adam is also an experienced live-television host and was previously a presenter on the world's longest-running kids TV programme, *Blue Peter*. Adam is ecstatic to bring his first book, *Adam Wins the Internet*, to life, and hopes to encourage readers with a story about something that every young person aspires to achieve – winning the internet! Who wouldn't?!

James Lancett is a London-based illustrator, director and yellow-sock lover! He is known for his illustrations for *Lightning Girl* by Alesha Dixon, the Avengers Assembly graphic novels, the Max Einstein series by James Patterson, and many others.